D0561101

HUMMER

HUMMER

Linda Gruenberg

Houghton Mifflin Company
Boston   1990

Library of Congress Cataloging-in-Publication Data

Gruenberg, Linda.
    Hummer / Linda Gruenberg.
        p. cm.
    Summary: When an elderly man agrees to let twelve-year-old Hummer
train his Arabian horse for a competitive trail ride, it is the one
bright spot in her difficult life living with a mentally ill mother
and a father who won't recognize the problem.
    ISBN 0-395-51080-5
    [1. Horses—Fiction. 2. Mentally ill—Fiction.] I. Title.
PZ7.G93245Hu 1990   89-38602
[Fic]—dc20   CIP
                           AC

J $b\delta T(5\mid$ $8/9D$

Printed in the United States of America

BP 10 9 8 7 6 5 4 3 2 1

For Dan, who wrote the first paragraph,
and for R. Dirk Jellema

HUMMER

ONE

They called her Hummer because she did. All the time. Well, at least whenever she was thinking of horses, which is pretty close to saying all the time. She was skinny and tough, if just a bit too pale, and she would sit in her classroom in the sixth grade and twist her shoulder-length brown hair and think of horses, and hum.

But now she wasn't humming. The scar on her lip where she once got bit by a dog was pale and trembling ever so slightly, and she sat on the school bus three-quarters of the way back trying not to cry. Hummer could feel the pebbled green vinyl seat and the window vibrating, and she could see the driver looking up in the big mirror over his head. The windows were open and the kids were yelling and Hummer could smell the water in the ditches and the dust and the barns and the fields. It was almost summer and school would soon be out. But she was still miserable.

Finally the bus stopped and the boys who lived by the Auroraville store got off.

"Bye, Pig Pen!" one of them shouted up at Hummer's open window.

Only Mary Lou, who lived at the end of the bus route, and Hummer, whose stop was next to last, were left. Mary Lou smiled at her, or rather grimaced, showing all her straight white teeth, but Hummer just swallowed hard and stared out the window. Being nice only when no one else was around seemed worse than always being mean.

It wouldn't have been so bad if what they said wasn't true. Especially the part about her dad sleeping in the barn and the house being filthy. Of course, none of them knew for sure about the house because her ma never let anyone in, but she still didn't want them guessing it.

Hummer knew that it wasn't the kids at school getting to her today, though. It was what had happened last night. Even just thinking about it sent shivers up and down Hummer's spine. She still wasn't sure whether the whole thing was real or not. That a storm had brewed up she was certain. She could almost feel the rolling of thunder and see the flashes of lightning that had shocked her awake. The rain had come down in torrents and lulled her half asleep again when she began dreaming.

In the dream, a horse galloped back and forth along a fence line, bolting in terror with each new crash of thunder. The horse's eyes rolled in panic and its frenzied heartbeat throbbed through Hummer's dream with a heavy bass. It let out a screaming nicker, and Hummer sat straight up, eyes open wide.

She heard the horse whinny again, and she sprang out of bed. Without changing from her nightgown, she fumbled with a pair of green rubber boots for a moment and finally pulled them up on the wrong feet. Trembling, she slipped on a jacket and scrunched a cowboy hat on her head as she ran from the bedroom, down the stairs, and through a narrow path amid stacks of garbage that led to the back door.

Outside, she didn't slow down. Mucking through the dark, sloppy barnyard, Hummer hiked up her nightgown in one hand and flailed the other for balance. The cry of a horse sounded from beyond the barn, and Hummer could faintly hear the pounding of hooves. She sucked in her breath. Those hoofbeats were real.

Hummer ran, not toward the sound, but to the barn. Skirting the milkhouse where her dad would be asleep on a cot, Hummer slipped into the barn and flipped on a far light. She grabbed a bucket and emptied corn into it from the storage room, caught up a bridle from a nail on the dusty wall, and then ran past the cows in the holding pen to the stall at the far end of the barn where a pony stood watching her come. His bright eyes stared in wonder at the startling figure she made. The skirt of her nightgown flew around her, and the clumsy wrong-footed boots made her trip once and flounder about

3

with the bucket. The pony began chewing in expectation of the corn.

"Mike," Hummer called as she threw open his stall door. "Mike, come on. You've got to help me catch a horse." She knew that the horse would be lured by another four-legger, even if it was just an old swaybacked pony. She slipped the bridle over Mike's ears and said, "The corn isn't for you." He had already confiscated a large mouthful. Then Hummer got on the pony's back, the nightgown pulled up to her knees and her mouth pressed into a determined line.

Outside, the moon was an eerie blue through the drizzle, and Hummer thought, No wonder the horse is scared. Even Mike was reluctant to plunge into the mist. She urged him toward the spot where she thought she had heard the horse, keeping such a tight hold on a handful of thick mane that her fingers began to cramp. The bucket rested in front of her leg on Mike's shoulder, making a creak-creak sound every time he took a step.

Mike found a cow path and followed it. Hummer huddled on his bare back, soaking wet, feeling the cold on her knees and the dark pressing in around her. She wondered if maybe she was the crazy one, not her mother, and if maybe her imagination had fooled her into thinking that a silly old dream was real only because she had been wanting a horse for so long.

Hummer really did need a horse. Mike was getting too old even for short trail rides. He began wheezing up any slight incline. She still rode him in the yard some, but he was awfully stiff to do the things she tried to teach him. He could sidepass and pivot, but the only ones who were around to notice were the cows. Holsteins were hard to impress.

As they reached the fence line, Hummer sensed the woods looming near. Beyond the pasture was nothing but trees and thick swamp. Nothing but cold and dark and wet.

Even squinting her eyes she couldn't see the slightest trace of the barn through the thick fog. She didn't know what to do. She could no longer hear the horse.

As Mike came into the swale that marked the corner of the pasture, an owl hooted from somewhere, and at the same moment a horse snorted loudly, almost a whistle. Hummer jumped, startled, and Mike nickered.

The mare was right there, on the other side of the fence. She danced sideways a step, blowing through her nostrils at Hummer and Mike, her neck curved high in the air and her ears strained forward. She was black, or dark brown, with a white blaze down her face, which seemed fluorescent against the moon. Even through the dark and the foggy drizzle, Hummer could see she was no ordinary horse.

Hummer spoke gently, shaking the bucket of corn. "Steady there, pretty fox." She slid off Mike and slipped through the fence with the bucket. "Easy does it. Whoa now." The mare shied back for an instant, and then stepped up again, reaching forward to blow into Hummer's face. Her breath was warm. A moment later, she plunged her head into the bucket. The corn crunched.

Hummer looked in wonder at the mare's wet ears, then cautiously gave her forelock a shake. "You're soaking wet," she said. She gently pulled the mare's ears, ringing water out, before she put the rope around her neck, trying not to tangle it in her mane.

They had to take the long way around to get back to the barn, Mike trailing along inside the fence. Twice the mare got spooked and nearly jerked the rope out of Hummer's hands, but finally they reached the gate and Hummer coaxed the mare through it.

When they arrived at the barn, Hummer put Mike and the mare in the stall together with some fresh hay.

"Good night, Mike," she said. "Good night, Fox."

Not bothering with any lights, Hummer crept into the milkhouse, hearing the familiar whoosh, whoosh, of the big paddles rotating in the milk cooler. She felt her way to the cot and, kneeling on the smooth cement, shook her dad's arm.

"Dad," she whispered loudly. "I caught a horse. It's a black mare, I think an Arabian, that doesn't belong to anybody."

"Huh?" Virgil moaned and rolled over.

"She was just running out there free."

His eyes blinked open. "What are you doing out here?"

6

"A horse. I caught a horse. I'm going to teach her to jump, and ride her at shows and stuff."

"You're soaking wet."

"It's raining out. There was a storm and that's how I found her, because she was scared and kept galloping back and forth at the fence line. I thought I was dreaming."

"It's a black Arab mare?"

"Uh huh."

"Old Man Riley."

"What?"

"Likely his horse. He's been looking for her since Tuesday. Said she jumped the fence. We'll get her back to him tomorrow."

"I was going to teach her to jump and to drive. I could ride her at the fair," Hummer said.

"You won't teach her nothing. Old Riley, he don't let anybody touch that horse. Go back to bed."

"I could ride her in parades."

"Good night, Hummer." He squeezed her hand.

Hummer slept so late the next morning that she almost missed the school bus. Fox would probably be gone when she got home and she couldn't even see the mare again because she didn't know where Riley lived. All she knew about the old man was that he usually ate at the truck stop and that he used to ride the rodeo. She didn't even know if Riley was his first or last name. She had never talked to him. Wouldn't have dared. Her dad said he was a hard man.

The tears began welling up again, and now Mary Lou was looking at her funny. Hummer tried smiling.

"Doing anything this weekend?" Mary Lou asked, not entirely innocently.

"Oh, Ma is probably taking me shopping," Hummer answered.

"You do that every weekend," Mary Lou said through her rows of white teeth. "You must have a lot of clothes by now."

Hummer shifted in the seat and nodded, picking at the hem of her sweater. She was glad it was almost her stop.

TWO

From the outside, the Ensings' house was ordinary, big and white and square, with two stories and a front porch like other farmhouses. It lay among some poplars – big quivering ones – alongside a gravel road. Two silos stood tall by the barn, and a corncrib, half empty, crouched near the shed between the two buildings. When the wind blew, which was often, the leaves on the trees would rustle and blink from light to dark to light green again.

As soon as the school bus turned the final corner before her house, Hummer watched through the dusty windows for Mike. She did that every day. First, she would see the red and white tops of the silos, then the trees and the barn, and last, the pasture. Every day when the pony heard the bus lumbering around the curve he would trot to the fence, head bobbing from the stiffness in his old legs. Today was different. Fox cantered behind him. Hummer couldn't believe her eyes.

Even through the bus window from down the road,

Hummer could see how proudly the mare carried herself, neck arched and tail flying. She occasionally swerved and bucked, kicking up dirt and feigning a nip at Mike to get him to play. Mike was more interested in the apple he knew Hummer would bring.

Hummer swung through the door of the bus almost the same instant it crumpled open. Throwing her books down in the spongy spring grass, she ran to the corral fence and slipped between the strands of wire. Mike nickered low in his throat. Fox snorted.

"Hello, bears," Hummer said, smiling. She pulled the apple from her bulging sweater pocket and held on to it tightly as Mike broke off the first half. "How come you're still here, Fox? Because you like it?" The mare reached forward, nuzzling Hummer for the rest of the apple. "I do too." She gave Fox the fruit. "Most of the time." The two horses chewed and slobbered, nodding their heads because the apple was sour.

Hummer stood with the animals, smiling and humming, stroking Fox, and wondering why Riley hadn't come to get her yet. Maybe he didn't have any way of getting her home and he needed someone to ride her there for him. Or maybe he didn't even want her back. That was a possibility. She climbed through the fence and gathered up her books, looking back at Fox. "I'll be back soon as I do chores," she promised.

Out of habit, Hummer held her breath as she swung open the screen door and walked through the porch into the house. She didn't breathe until the living room, and then her nostrils curled at the smell of rotten eggs. She swallowed hard.

Her mother sat in front of the TV in an old wooden rocking chair. All about her, against the walls and built up around the TV, were boxes and garbage bags, some of them spilling out old milk cartons and tin cans. Haphazard stacks of newspapers filled one corner, two of which had fallen over into the garbage.

The house had not always been so bad. Hummer remembered only a year ago when she'd been able to spread her schoolbooks out over the living room floor, but since then the garbage had taken over. There wasn't any floor to work on now.

Still, she was used to the mess. It wasn't that she didn't care, just that it had begun to seem like the normal thing. After the first few breaths you really didn't notice the smell.

Leona looked up from the TV as Hummer came in. "Hi, dolly," she said. "Are you home from school already?"

"Um hmm. We played kickball at recess and I got picked first." She wished she had been picked first. She wished she had been picked at all.

"That's nice."

"Um hmm. Did you see the mare out in the pasture?"

"What?"

"I caught me a horse last night. Dad says she belongs to old man Riley."

"That's nice. Listen, dolly. Tell your dad I'm not coming out to help milk tonight."

"Okay. She's a real pretty horse. One white sock and a little skinny blaze down her face, like a racing stripe. She's dark brown. Almost black." She paused. "Riley doesn't want her anymore."

"I really don't think I could go out," Leona answered. "I've got such pains in my legs today. Tell your dad that."

"Okay."

When Leona looked back toward the TV, Hummer turned around and ran up the stairs, two at a time.

She came back down dressed in her barn clothes. On her way through the kitchen, she located the rotten eggs, picked them up, checked to make sure Leona wasn't looking, then walked across the road by the mailbox to throw the whole mess into the ditch. She pulled out the contents of the mailbox – a phone bill and a grain bill – and headed for the barn.

The barn door stood open, and a light shone faintly from inside where her dad would already be milking. Hummer followed the familiar thub-*dub*, thub-*dub*, of the milking machine into the milkhouse and cracked open the door to the milking parlor. Virgil stood in the pit, steamy water running down his elbows as he washed the bags of the row of four cows who had just come in. The batch of cows on the opposite side still had milkers on, though Hummer could see they were almost done. She walked softly in front of the first batch

12

down into the pit. Her dad acknowledged her with a nod as she waved the mail at him and set it carefully on top of the paper towel dispenser. She took some paper towels and began drying the cows he had just washed.

"Did you just come from the house?" he asked. His voice was low, so as not to disturb the cows.

Hummer nodded. "Ma said to tell you she isn't gonna help with chores tonight."

Virgil looked up.

"Her legs hurt."

"She'll probably be out tomorrow night," Virgil answered, "soon as she feels better." Every night he said the same thing. Every night Leona had a different reason not to come out. Virgil sighed, then began finishing up the first batch of cows, gently pulling down on each milker before he took it off, to squeeze out the last few squirts of milk.

"What about the mare?" Hummer asked.

"Riley's coming by after chores. It's his horse all right."

"Right after chores?"

"Dunno, but he sure was glad somebody caught her. She's worth a bundle. Just don't go fooling around with his horse now and make him mad, you hear? Riley ain't nobody to mess around with, or his horse either, the way it sounds." Virgil slopped orange teat dip on the finished cows, and Hummer swung the front gate open to let them out.

"Giddup, Bessy." Virgil prodded the first cow in the

ribs. They all sauntered out, licking their noses for the last bits of grain as another batch came in to take their place. Virgil started over again with the hose and steamy water on the new batch. "Don't slam the door on your way out."

Hummer adjusted a squeaking milker and then left the parlor, closing the door softly behind her. It was important not to startle the cows.

She left the milkhouse carrying three big calf bottles under one arm, and a full bucket of milk, stiff-armed, on the other, swaying as she walked to balance it all. She could hear the calves bleating from the far end of the barn. They thought they were starving. Twice a day they thought they were starving.

The biggest calves drank their milk from a trough, but Hummer fed the ten littlest by hand. They could be tricky. They'd pull and push and butt against each other and switch places until it was hard to tell which calves had been fed. It didn't matter how they fought though, she always fed them in the same order so she wouldn't forget anybody.

Three calves at a time got their bottles, while the others sucked on everything they could reach, including each others' ears and Hummer's fingers. Usually Hummer played with them after they'd been fed, but tonight she was in a hurry. She wanted to brush Fox before Riley came to take her away. As fast as she could, Hummer refilled the bottles and finished the calves.

14

When she had scrubbed out the calf bottles, Hummer brought Mike and Fox in from pasture. She knotted together a binder-twine halter for Fox and led the two outside and tied them to the hitching post. Mike pulled against his rope for grass, his lips slapping in a futile attempt to reach the tops of some tall weeds.

Fox stood quietly, lowering her head as Hummer curried and brushed her rough coat. She had the most beautiful eyes Hummer had ever seen. They were big and deep and black-looking, and when the sun shone into them, as it was doing now, Hummer could see a blue-violet square of light in the center of the darkness. They were strong eyes that didn't look away or blink. Hummer thought she could see all the way into the mare's soul through them.

"I wish," Hummer told Fox slowly, "that you were mine." She smoothed the mare's forelock down the middle of her wide forehead and sighed. She couldn't imagine any problem so big that having a horse wouldn't solve. Especially a horse like Fox.

Everything would probably start solving itself with Fox around, Hummer thought. Leona would surely start coming out of the house again to watch Hummer ride, and Virgil would want to take them to horse shows.

Humming softly, she untangled and smoothed and stroked until Fox looked more as if she belonged in a show ring than tied to a hitching post outside a dairy barn.

When Hummer finished, she untied the mare and led her up the driveway. The poplar tree by the fence became a judge, and Hummer paraded the mare past it. The mare trotted in big strides, pulling against the halter, arching her neck. Hummer smiled broadly over her shoulder at the tree. She stopped Fox and stood her up, moving her back and forth until all four feet were square.

"Good girl. Good baby," she crooned. Remembering herself, she bowed to the tree and smiled again. The mare nuzzled her and Hummer gently pulled her ears. "Come on, Fox-Fox." They returned to the hitching post.

Hummer looked up the road as far as she could see. No truck and horse trailer. She overturned a bucket and set it down beside Fox. She stood on it and looked up the road again. It wouldn't do for Riley to catch her on his horse. She leaned over the mare's back a little, and when Fox didn't seem troubled by it, she jumped the rest of the way on and slung her leg over. Fox started, shooting her head up. Hummer felt her stomach go queasy when she realized how far down the ground was. Fox was much taller than Mike.

"Easy baby. Easy does it." Hummer stroked the mare's neck, humming and smoothing her mane, until Fox settled down again. "I bet you haven't been ridden in a while, huh? Well, come on, it's okay." She leaned forward, and hanging on to the mare's mane with one hand, untied the rope from the hitching post with the

16

other. She slowly sat back up, the rope in her hand. "Not much of a bridle," she said to Fox, "but then we're not going much of anywhere." She clicked loudly and put her heels to the mare's sides.

Fox lunged forward in a canter, and Hummer grabbed her mane to keep from sliding off. She pulled back on the rope as the mare cantered faster and faster toward the road. "Whoa, Fox," Hummer called out, her voice rising high in fear. The mare only sped up.

For an instant Hummer steeled herself to jump, but then the idea of Fox loose again made her cling tighter. She tried turning Fox, but nothing happened until she laid the rope over the mare's mane, neck-reining her. Fox turned so quickly that Hummer was aware of hanging in the air before she landed on the ground with a thud.

Fox cantered back to Mike at the hitching post and, before she had time to wonder where she hurt, Hummer was on her feet running after her. As Hummer caught the lead rope in relief, she saw how the whites of the mare's eyes showed and she could see the sheen of nervous sweat on her coat. Fox breathed air in great gasps that made her sides heave and looked back at Hummer.

"Sorry," Hummer said, her voice coming out all funny and shaky. She had fallen off before, but only from Mike.

The mare watched Hummer with one wide eye. Even when her breathing had calmed and her pulse slowed down, she held her neck curved in a high arch. Hummer watched Fox too, wondering if her own eyes looked as wild.

Then Hummer realized what the problem was. She had been trying to ride a hot-blooded mare as if she were an old lazy pony. Carefully, carefully, Hummer moved the bucket to Fox's side again, and, knees still shaking, slipped onto her warm back. "Easy, Fox the fox."

This time she gave only a soft cluck with her tongue, and Fox trotted. Hummer grew calmer as she guided Fox warily in a circle. She rode the horse around the poplar trees in the yard, clinging to her mane and bouncing slightly to her trot. Mike stood at the hitching post watching, having given up getting grass on his own. The sun had sunk just below the horizon.

A truck door slammed, and it startled Fox into a canter.

"What do you think you're doing?" a voice called out. An old blue truck and rust-colored horse trailer were in the driveway.

"Whoa," Hummer said to Fox. "Whoa. Stop." The mare slowed down some, and Hummer jumped off, stumbling in the soft grass. She pulled Fox into a circle to get her to stop. "Easy bear. Walk now." With one hand in the mare's mane she led Fox toward Riley, her knees shaking again. He looked mad. She couldn't believe she had forgotten to watch for him.

"I said, What do you think you're doing?"

"Riding," Hummer answered in a whisper.

"Oh, I see. You catch somebody's loose horse and you think it's a free-for-all. You coulda got yourself killed. That ain't no kid's pony."

Hummer opened her mouth but no words came out. She felt tears welling up for the second time that day.

"Did you hear me? That horse coulda thrown you higher than St. Peter's sandals." He held out a gnarled hand for the end of the rope. Hummer gave it to him, staring at her feet and keeping one hand tangled in the mare's mane. Fox stood still, blowing through her wide nostrils and looking from one person to the other. Mike nickered from the hitching post.

"Virgil's girl, are you?" Riley asked suddenly.

"Um hmm."

"You the one that caught her?"

"Um hmm."

"Well, speak up."

Silence.

Riley spit a string of tobacco into the gravel of the driveway and cleared his throat. "Like my horse, do you?"

"Um hmm."

"She's a purebred – name is Roxie. I've had her for, let's see now, nigh onto six years. Got her when she was only three months old."

"Really?" Hummer looked up for the first time. Riley didn't look as mean as she had thought at first. Just old. His back was stooped, and his hands and face looked

19

like wrinkled-up old leather. He wore old, soft work pants and a faded red plaid shirt. "What do you call her for short?"

"Don't call her nothing for short, just Roxie. Had her broke when she was three. She ain't been rode since then." He fingered the rough binder-twine halter, stroking Fox's face with the back of his fingers. "Guess she didn't buck you off."

"She's spirited," Hummer said.

Riley nodded, looking pleased. "No, that's one thing she ain't, is short on spirit. It's a wonder you could hold her at all in this get-up." He tugged on the binder twine of the halter. "Reckon you're quite a little horse-woman."

Hummer felt her face color. "I call her Fox," she said.

Riley sucked in his breath and his lips showed the outline of his gums, where his teeth should have been. "Fox, short for Roxie, eh?"

Hummer nodded, staring at her feet. "She's got such bright fox eyes. You know?" She felt stubborn, as though it were an important point.

Riley grunted. "That your pony?" He was looking at Mike.

"Um hmm. His name is Mike."

"Take good care of him, do you?"

"Um hmm."

"Does he know anything?"

"You want to see him?"

20

"Yeah. Bring him on out."

Hummer left Riley holding Fox and ran into the barn for Mike's bridle. Her dad had finished milking and was hosing down the parlor. She opened the door and yelled in to him, "Riley's here," then let it slam again.

By the time she had Mike bridled, Virgil stood out on the lawn with Riley, both men watching her. "Let's see what you can do with him," Riley said.

Hummer urged Mike into a trot, stroking his neck with the back of her fingers. Mike felt small and clumsy beneath her compared to the mare. His old legs were stiff.

She cued him for the canter with one heel, making a wide circle in the lawn. Hummer could see Riley and her dad conferring about something. She wished she could hear what they were saying.

It seemed like ages before the old man called for them to come back. Hummer eased Mike into a gentle stop and stroked his neck. "Good boy," she whispered. They walked to where Virgil and Riley stood.

"Good pony," Riley said. He patted Mike. "Getting old, ain't he?"

Hummer nodded. Fox and Mike nuzzled each other.

Virgil cleared his throat. "Riley was just saying he'd leave his mare here for a week or so if you wanted to ride her. Just to give her a little exercise."

Riley spit his tobacco again. "If you want, that is."

21

THREE

Leona stank. Her housedress could scarcely strain around her huge body anymore, and she had stopped washing her hair. She rarely got up. She just sat in that big old rocking chair in front of the TV, sometimes rocking, sometimes not, sometimes staring at the TV without turning it on.

Saturday morning Hummer turned the TV on for Leona after doing her chores, and announced, "I'm going outside to ride Fox."

"Okay," Leona said. "Tell your dad I can't come out."

"I took a bath this morning," Hummer hinted.

"I really couldn't go out today."

"The towels are clean, too. We went to the Laundromat yesterday." She and Virgil did laundry every Friday night after chores.

"Okay, dolly."

Hummer sighed. She knew Leona wasn't going to take a bath. "I'm going out," she said.

Hummer's face was pinched into a frown as she let Fox into the barn from the pasture. Riley had left Fox's halter and bridle with Hummer, so now she slipped the loose halter over the mare's head and led her out to the hitching post in the yard.

As she brushed Fox, Hummer couldn't keep from worrying. Virgil didn't know how bad Leona was getting. He didn't go in the house anymore, so he didn't see her.

Hummer remembered when he lived in the house. She used to wake up in the morning to the sound of his buzzing electric razor. Now he shaved in the tiny bathroom next to the milkhouse and washed himself from the sink. When there were groceries, like toothpaste, bananas, and the eggs he kept buying, she carried them into the house herself.

When she'd brushed Fox's tail out so not a snarl would catch as she ran her fingers through it, she divided it into three long strands and began braiding. Hummer pulled the rubber band out of her own ponytail, then twisted it around the end of the braid in Fox's tail.

She hummed as she braided Fox's mane into as many tiny braids as she could, tying the rest with string. Then she heard the sound of the rattling old truck.

Fox nickered and Hummer looked down the road, straining to see if Riley had the horse trailer. He didn't. Hummer hugged Fox's neck, knowing she could keep her for at least another day, then swung onto the mare's

23

bare back. Fox tossed her head and began backing up, and when Hummer urged her forward, pranced sideways instead.

"Easy does it." She stroked the mare's neck and, when they were both calm again, urged the mare toward Riley's truck. Riley shut off the engine in the shade of a big poplar tree and rolled down the window.

"Giving ya a hard time?" Riley asked. Then to Hummer's surprise, he began a deep rumbling laugh.

She stared at him.

Pointing at the braids in Fox's mane, Riley shook with laughter that nearly became a hacking cough. "Never seen her prettied up like that before," he said. "Downright embarrassing." Then he stopped laughing. There were tears by his eyes and he wiped at them.

Hummer smiled, sort of, wondering if it was good or bad to make Riley laugh. She didn't know what to say. She kept Fox beside the truck window until Riley finally motioned with his hand for them to get out and ride. Hummer turned Fox away in relief. It was much easier to ride than to talk.

Hummer didn't canter Fox at first. With Riley watching, she didn't want to fall off again. If he thought she couldn't ride well enough, he might take Fox back. Hummer practiced making the mare trot slow, then fast, then slow, then in big circles and little circles, then making square corners and smooth stops. She knew Riley would approve of that. If he approved of anything.

When Hummer finally slid off Fox's back, her jeans

were wet and scratchy. She pulled at them while she led Fox in a circle to cool off. That was the problem with riding bareback. Horses sweat a lot.

Hummer led Fox toward Riley's pickup, wondering what he had thought of her riding, but saw that Riley had started the engine and was backing up. He didn't even wait to say goodbye. Hummer wanted to ask him if he would mind her riding Fox in the woods, but she didn't dare yell for him to stop. He pulled out of the driveway with a crunch of wheels on gravel. Hummer waved her arm in a wide arc, but Riley didn't see her until he was down the road a ways. Then he lifted a hand in the window.

Every day it was the same, and Hummer never did dare ask him about riding in the woods. He didn't say much, except once he advised Hummer to hold her head higher when she rode. "You ain't got nothing to be ashamed of when you're on *my* horse," he said. "Don't be so scared to hold your chin up." Hummer nodded and did what he said. She didn't feel so shy after that, and felt pleased to have someone watching her ride.

One evening after chores but before her ride, Hummer was sitting on the bottom step of the porch when her dad walked up to the house.

Virgil tucked in his shirttail, working all the way around his pants several times, and knocked on the screen door before he opened it. "Leona? Leona, you in here?"

Hummer heard a shuffling sound and then the creak of the inner door opening. Leona stood in one threshold and Virgil in the other, and it looked as though they thought something bad might happen if they both got onto the porch at the same time.

"Don't come in!" Leona warned. "I'm not ready."

"Thought you might wanna come out," Virgil said.

"What for?" Leona opened the door wider. "I'm not doing chores tonight; I've got such aches in my knees."

"Old Riley's coming over to watch Hummer ride the horse, and I thought you might like watching too. If you want. Riley'll be here and all."

Hummer felt her heart beat fast. Having Fox around was already making things better.

"What'll I wear?" Leona finally asked.

"What'll you wear? Well, wear just what you got on." She was wearing a housedress. "Or anything you want. But Riley oughta be here soon, and Hummer ain't gonna be riding all night."

"Maybe my blue skirt," Leona said. "Or do you think my green one?"

"Ain't nobody gonna be out there but Hummer and Riley. Ain't no big deal."

"I think the green." The door creaked shut. "Or maybe the blue," she added dimly.

Virgil watched the door close, then turned and smiled at Hummer. His forehead was damp. "Your ma's gonna come watch you ride," he told her, although she already knew. "She's proud of you, just like me."

Hummer stood up to go back to the barn with Virgil.

"Guess I should ask her more often," Virgil said. "It'd be easier if she weren't so blame hard to talk to. She's probably just going through a stage." Virgil opened the milkhouse door for Hummer. "Women are always going through stages."

Hummer wondered if Mary Lou's mother went through stages. She didn't think so.

Riley had come and gone, and Hummer had finished riding when she and Virgil realized that Leona probably wasn't coming out.

"Looks like your ma changed her mind," Virgil said.

"Maybe you should ask her again," Hummer answered.

Virgil turned his cap around on his head. "She's probably watching TV. She probably had some program to watch, and she forgot about that when I asked her to come out."

"I'll finish hosing down the parlor, if you go see," Hummer said, watching her feet.

"Ain't nothing to see," Virgil said. "Just tell your ma good night for me when you go in." He turned back to the barn, and Hummer knew that was final.

In the house, Leona was in front of the TV, in the rocking chair. Hummer felt a surge of anger at her, and demanded, "What happened?"

"Oh, I couldn't go out. Not tonight, with my knees aching so."

"But you *said* you would." Hummer glared at her, then noticed how strangely she was dressed. Leona's blue skirt hung below the green one, and her house-dress was beneath all that. The elastic waistband of the green skirt was stretched to capacity.

"You got dressed up?" she asked tentatively.

"I've got a red dress, too," Leona said. "I don't know." Her voice trailed off in confusion.

"You didn't know which one to wear?"

Leona rocked the chair faster.

"Well, any one of them would be nice, by itself," Hummer said kindly.

"I really couldn't go out," Leona answered.

"It's okay," Hummer reassured her. "I just rode Fox, was all. I cantered her too, this time. I'm getting used to her. She's got real smooth gaits, like rocking in a rocking chair. I'm getting so I can sit to her trot."

"My back the way it is, I couldn't go out, could I?" Leona asked.

Hummer shook her head.

FOUR

The morning barn was unusually quiet. Hummer headed for the calf pens with her bottles of milk, yawning as she went through the big doors. A calf bawled. The noise made an echoing sound. Maybe the cows were all asleep. She opened her eyes and looked around. They weren't all asleep. They weren't even in the barn. She ran to the door of their run and looked out to pasture. No cows. Not even one.

She ran toward the parlor. The milking cows were where they belonged, lined up outside the parlor doors. Just the young stock and dry cows were gone. Hummer slipped through the parlor door. Virgil looked up. "Dad, the cows are out." She mouthed the words at him almost noiselessly.

"Goll darn it all," Virgil whispered. He scratched his head. "What'll be next?"

Hummer didn't look at her dad. She just stroked one of the cows and waited for a decision, knowing what it would be. Since she couldn't do the milking by herself, it would be up to her to round up the loose cows, wherever they were.

"Guess you better go find them," Virgil finally said. "Take Mike and be careful. Hope they ain't got too far."

Hummer nodded and slipped out of the parlor. She knew she should do what her dad said and take Mike, but instead, she grabbed Fox's bridle from the nail. Her heart skipped a beat as she did it, knowing that she didn't have permission from Riley, but with Fox around it seemed silly to take slow old Mike.

Fox and Mike both nickered when they saw Hummer coming toward their stall. They expected their morning ration of sweet feed. Hummer dumped the grain into their buckets, then remembered she had to get milk for Leona before she left. In the milkhouse, she carefully ran a pitcher full of creamy milk from the tap in the cooler.

Leona was just coming out of the bathroom when Hummer arrived in the house. "Good morning, dolly," she said.

"Morning." Hummer was relieved to see Leona back in her housedress. "I'm going to be gone for a while; I have to go round up the cows."

"Okay, dolly."

"Dad's upset about it, you know, the cows being out and all. But I'm going to ride Fox. Dad said take Mike, but Fox is so much quicker I think I should take her instead."

"Good idea," Leona agreed. "Tell your dad to get some milk for me."

"I already got it – it's in the kitchen. Fox can go farther, too. She won't get tired out like Mike. Riley won't mind."

"I think I should have cereal this morning."

"I have to go," Hummer said, already on her way out.

"Corn flakes, I think," Leona added.

"Bye," Hummer called as she went through the porch.

In the barn, Fox was done eating, so Hummer slipped the bridle over the mare's head. Mike whinnied as they left and Hummer felt a pang of guilt for leaving him behind, but when she realized that she wasn't having any trouble handling Fox, she felt better again. Riding her every day had already done some good.

It was easy to see where the stock had gotten out. The fence in the corner by the swale was trampled, and cow tracks made a wide swath into the swamp. The manure in the path was already old, so Hummer knew the cows must have been out for most of the night. She wondered what had spooked them.

The mare trotted, following the path, and broke to a walk only when the brush got so thick she had to push her way through it. The cows had circled the boggy part of the swamp, but even so, they'd created some deep mud holes around the edges. Fox picked her way along, keeping out of the water as best she could.

Hummer wondered if Riley would be angry, having

his horse out here in the swamp with deer flies swarming around. She broke a poplar branch to swish the flies away and it worked pretty well. The last thing she wanted to do was make Riley angry.

When the path of the cows cut out of the woods and onto a dirt road, Fox shook her head and pulled down against the bit. She wanted to run. Hummer grabbed a handful of mane just in time. Fox burst forward, bucked once, shied at an old tree stump, and galloped along the edge of the road.

It wasn't Hummer who noticed where the cows turned into the woods again, but Fox. She cut abruptly into the ditch, sniffed at some cow manure, and followed the cloven hoof prints up a hill. The tracks were looking fresher all the time. Hummer sat back up and wondered how Fox knew they were supposed to be following the cows.

At last the bushes crackled and rustled and the low mooing of a forlorn cow floated out from somewhere. Fox's ears cocked forward and she turned and nickered. Hummer thought she heard a calf bawl; she shook her head and listened harder. There weren't any calves with them. The calves had all been in their pens where they belonged. Fox snorted and whinnied again. The strays were in a circle of trees.

Hummer counted fifteen dry cows and seven yearlings and sighed with relief. They were all there. Something seemed to be wrong though.

A calf cried again.

32

Then Hummer saw that one of the cows had a string of afterbirth hanging from under her tail. Near her legs lay a tiny black calf.

Hummer slid off Fox's back and tied her to a tree. She approached the calf slowly to keep from frightening the cow. This was the smallest calf Hummer had ever seen. She knelt down and touched its fuzzy neck. It was a heifer.

The calf bleated sadly. The mother cow mooed and bunted at the baby with her nose, but the tiny one wouldn't stand. Her eyes were dull and mosquitos coated her body. Hummer wanted to rock the tiny calf like a baby. Instead she looped her arms under the calf's belly and pulled her to her feet.

Still the calf wouldn't stand.

"Put your feet down," Hummer told her, but the calf just crumpled her knees. Hummer lowered the baby to the ground and nuzzled her nose into the damp neck. She smelled so newborn and sweet.

"You're an early one," Hummer said. "Too early. And you aren't gonna live long unless you get something to eat." She took a deep breath and lifted the calf again, pushing its tiny nose toward the cow's bag. The cow licked at her baby's tail, mooing softly. "Take just one little drink," Hummer advised. "Come on." The calf was heavier than she looked. Finally she took a nipple, and her mouth twitched.

Hummer slipped a finger between the calf's lips and stroked the wet ridges on the roof of its mouth. She had

33

seen her dad do that before. It worked. The calf began sucking.

"Thataway." Hummer shifted arms. "Just one little drink." The calf pulled on a teat half-heartedly, and foamy milk trickled down her muzzle.

Hummer wondered how far they were from home. Seven or eight miles maybe. Too far for a newborn calf to go, especially a sick newborn.

The calf was sucking a little harder now, and some life had come into her eyes. Hummer's arms ached and she shifted her position again. The back of her knee itched.

Finally, the calf stopped drinking, and Hummer let her down to the ground. Fox stomped and snorted and circled once around the tree. "Just a minute, Fox," Hummer said. She stroked the calf and patted the mama cow's wide sides. "You're gonna be okay."

It wasn't easy getting the calf onto Fox's back. The mother cow mooed and complained and bellowed, and Hummer had to slap her and push her away. Hummer pointed the calf's front feet up and pushed her at the mare's back. It might have worked, but every time Hummer got her lifted, Fox would shy sideways and snort, the whites of her eyes showing, and then Hummer had to drop the calf again. The rest of the cows stared, rubbing their heads on each other, swishing their tails and stamping their feet.

It seemed like a long time before the heifer hung limp and heavy on Fox's back. She didn't struggle at all. Fox seemed to understand at last what Hummer was doing, and she turned her head around to sniff her new passenger. Hummer patted the mare with forgiveness and scrambled onto her back behind the newborn.

Getting the cows started back was not as much trouble as Hummer thought it might be. She didn't have to cut or chase them at all. The mother cow followed Fox, mooing to her baby with every stride, and the others stayed close behind.

It was a long trip home. The inside of Hummer's legs felt raw from all the sweat and the rubbing, and they itched. The calf was miserable too, and at first bleated sadly. Hummer was happy that at least the calf felt good enough to complain. Later on, she didn't even bleat.

The sun had slipped into the afternoon by the time they pushed through the swamp and saw the farm fence. New barbed wire had been stretched tight between the old fence posts where the cows had trampled it down, so Hummer had to lead the cows the long way around.

Virgil and Riley had seen them coming and were standing by the fence. Hummer didn't look at Riley; she suddenly remembered he might be mad at her. Her dad swung the gate open wide and the cows didn't need any prompting to get into their pasture. They headed for the fresh hay. Only the mama cow stayed behind, mooing to her calf.

"What've we got here?" Virgil asked. He took the calf down from Fox's back and held her, one arm around the chest and one under the rump. "Heifer calf? She's plenty early."

Hummer nodded.

"She might make it," Virgil said, "if we get a little milk in her and a shot of penicillin." He squinted up at Hummer. "It must have been quite a job getting her up on that horse." Then he headed for the barn with the calf, the mother cow following.

Hummer glanced sideways at Riley as she slid down from Fox's back. Her legs stung, but she saw with relief that Riley wasn't angry. His lips were sucked into his mouth in a funny sort of half smile.

"Had to take her through a swamp," Hummer said to him, "and there was a lot of brush and stuff." She watched his face, waiting for him to say something. Fox rubbed her head on Hummer's shoulder, scratching herself and knocking Hummer back with each rub. Hummer slipped the bridle over the mare's ears. "The bugs were pretty bad."

Riley put a hand under Fox's jaw. "Guess if you can ride her through the bushes for a day chasing after cows and then get a calf on her back you ain't doing half bad."

Hummer finally smiled at him and clicked to Fox to walk. They led the mare into the back of the barn and gave her hay and a good rubdown. Fox could have water later when she had cooled off.

FIVE

The new calf quit drinking on Wednesday. Hummer tried to feed her before the school bus came, but the young heifer could hardly hold her own head up and no amount of coaxing would get her to suck. Hummer even tried pouring a little milk into the baby's mouth. She just choked. Then the school bus came around the corner, so Hummer had to run to the house for her books.

It was the last day of school.

She remembered what her dad had said about the calf. Yesterday Hummer had been sitting in the calf pen when he came in. The calf had been asleep. Virgil squatted beside them, ground his heel into the straw, and said, "She don't look too good to me."

They stared at the calf.

He cleared his throat. "You ain't named her, or nothing, have you?"

"No." Hummer fondled the calf's ear. It felt like silk.

He lifted the tiny head to look closer and wiggled a

finger into the heifer's mouth. "Nope. Good idea not to name her." He let the head down gently. "Sweet little thing, ain't she?"

Hummer had agreed.

Now she flung open the screen door of the house and grabbed her books off the chair before she ran back to the bus. Hummer guessed that if her dad didn't have any more hope than that, then there wasn't much hope.

The weather looked just as lousy as Hummer felt. The sky hung heavy and low. Hummer knew how excited everyone at school would be, it being the last day, while she'd have to sit through it all wondering whether or not the calf had died.

Mrs. Pace handed out crossword puzzles the first thing, which Hummer quietly worked on, but later, when everyone was supposed to be cleaning out desks, Larry leaned over and started whispering questions at her.

"Heard you took a trip to Europe," he said.

Hummer nodded and turned back as though she were busy. She carefully brushed together little pieces of pencil shavings, then took the handful to the front of the room to the wastebasket.

Larry pulled on the hood of her sweater as soon as she came back. "How'd you get there? Swim?"

Mrs. Pace looked up and then back down at her book. That was her warning signal.

Hummer wished she'd never started that thing about Europe. She'd heard about one of the high school girls,

Kristi, who had gone there for Easter vacation, and after that Kristi got elected "most likely to succeed" and "prettiest smile" of the senior class. Hummer was sure that Europe had something to do with it. Or it could have been because of Kristi's funny new clothes and the French accent she had picked up. At any rate, Hummer thought that if she pretended she had gone to Europe, the same thing might happen to her.

Larry pulled her hood again. "How'd you get there, huh? Swim?" He puffed his cheeks out like a frog and pretended to do the breast stroke. Todd, who sat in front of Larry, giggled.

"We flew," Hummer hissed at him. She turned around again, this time with a bang of her notebook on the desk.

Mrs. Pace aimed another warning glance.

When Mrs. Pace had gone safely back to her book, Hummer scowled at Larry. She felt her face go hot.

"What'd you fly on, a broom?" Larry asked.

"Ya, ha, a broom?" Todd whispered, grinning. "Your ma let you all fly on her broom?"

Larry grabbed the end of a make-believe broomstick and rocked wildly back and forth. Half the class burst into laughter.

With that, Mrs. Pace finally stood up and the tittering stopped. Todd slunk down into his seat, and Hummer stared miserably at the floor. "That's enough," Mrs. Pace snapped. "Hummer, hush; Larry, you mind your own business. Everybody, heads down."

A wavelike groan made its way across the room.

"Come on. Heads down, right now. If you're not going to behave, I can always keep you occupied."

Hummer was glad to put her head on the desk. At least nobody could talk to her then.

Mrs. Pace went to the door. "Not a peep out of anybody," she said, "or you can spend all of your last afternoon with your heads down."

She opened the door and went out. The class didn't make a sound. Finally, a girl lifted her head up and looked around. "The coast is clear," she said. Others began looking up. Hummer did not.

"Thanks a lot," someone whispered sarcastically.

"Don't look at me," Larry said. "Look at Hummer. She's the one bragging about Europe."

"She probably doesn't even know where Europe is," someone said.

"Do so," Hummer said into the desk.

"Where then?"

"None of your business."

"How'd you get there?"

"Flew." Hummer looked up and sat up. Everyone was staring at her.

Larry started his witch imitation again, only quietly. "Your mother's a crazy witch, and you ain't never been to Europe," he said.

"Have so," Hummer said loudly. Her T-shirt was beginning to feel clammy.

"What'd you do there?" Mary Lou asked.

"Went shopping," Hummer said.

The class broke out laughing.

"Did so go there," Hummer yelled. She stood up when they laughed harder. "Did so go there and we're going back, too. We're going back there to live. I'm going to Spain to live on a horse farm and I'm going to school in Paris and –" She stopped.

Mrs. Pace was standing in the doorway. She looked furious. All the children quietly put their heads down on their desks, except Hummer. She found herself standing on the wrong side of the desk to get into it. She was the only one to be sent to the principal on the last day of school.

The door to Mr. Saxton's office stood open, and Hummer watched the top of his head for a moment as he wrote something on a piece of paper. She tapped on the doorjamb. The principal looked up and focused on her through his thick glasses.

"Ah, Henrietta," he said. "Come in." He smiled at her. "Sit down. Looks like we're going to get some rain," he said.

She sat down and stared miserably at the edge of a pencil holder printed with an old-fashioned map.

Mr. Saxton cleared his throat and leaned back, holding a pencil between his first two fingers.

"Henrietta," he began, "this isn't quite what it seems. I'm not here to yell at you, just to help you."

Hummer looked quickly up at him and back down.

"I know you've been having some trouble with something. And not just today. Mrs. Pace tells me you have a tendency to stretch the truth, to tell a few stories that aren't quite true. Though they may seem true to you at the time."

He paused, waiting for her to speak, but she didn't know how to answer that. It wasn't that she thought those things were true, really, just that she wanted them to be true.

"Do you believe your stories, when you tell them?" he asked. When Hummer didn't answer, he continued. "Henrietta, your mother hasn't been to a parent/teacher conference all year. Can you tell me about that?"

"She's just so busy," Hummer explained, suddenly talkative. "You know, church meetings and things. Shopping. And she travels a lot. To visit relatives, because we really have a lot of relatives." She looked up at Mr. Saxton, then quickly out the window. "Anyway, my dad likes to come," she added.

He followed her gaze. The first few drops of rain were splattering on the glass, and the sky looked black. It looked like a lot more rain was coming.

"We can help you, you know," he said, as though she hadn't answered his question. "If you need help, or if your mother needs help, we can get it, but you have to tell us. You have to tell somebody," he said invitingly.

For a moment Hummer wanted to tell him that her mother hadn't had a bath yet this month, and that the refrigerator was so full of old food it couldn't be used, which was why the eggs kept going bad. She even looked up at him to say those things, but her mouth just wouldn't open. She could think of what to say, but the words were too heavy to turn into sound.

Mr. Saxton sighed. "It's okay," he said. "Just take this advice; don't make it so hard for yourself. If you'd stop trying so hard to impress people, you'd have an easier time." He turned in his chair to watch the rain on the window. "Next year," he said, "you'll be in the middle school. New people, new classes. It will be a lot easier on you if you don't get off to a bad start." He smiled at Hummer again, so she tried to look friendly too.

"Was there anything you wanted to say?" he asked.

When she shook her head, he went on. "Then you might as well go back to your class. Have a nice summer, Henrietta."

"Thanks," Hummer answered, jumping up quickly from the chair. "Bye."

Hummer walked back to her class slowly. She thought over what he had said, trying to think how it could help her. "You have to tell somebody," he had said, but what exactly would she tell them? If she told somebody her mother was going strange, that wouldn't be the whole story. After all, her dad kept buying groceries that had no place to go. He gave her sacks of things to carry into the house that only added to the mess.

And even if she told someone, what would they do? She imagined all three of them, Leona, Virgil, and herself, wearing white pajamas in a mental hospital. At home, Fox would jump the fence and run away.

She wondered what had happened to make Leona act so crazy, but she couldn't think of anything. Maybe nothing had happened; maybe she'd always been a little strange. Hummer wasn't sure.

Mr. Saxton had been right about the weather. By the time the bus stopped at Hummer's house after school, the rain was coming down in torrents. To her surprise, Riley's truck was parked in the driveway. He usually didn't come until after chore time, when he knew she'd have time to ride.

The bus door folded open and Hummer jumped out onto the wet driveway, holding her notebook on top of her head as a shield from the rain. Through the water-blurred windows of Riley's truck she could see the old man in the cab, his head against the back of the seat and his hat tipped down.

Hummer ran toward the house, the rain pelting her face, but as she approached the truck, Riley's form straightened and a hand pushed his hat up. He knocked on the window at her. She stopped and stared in at him, wondering what to do next. Riley jerked a thumb at the passenger side door and leaned across the seat to push it open. She climbed in, shook her notebook, and blew the water off her upper lip.

"Rainin' like a cow pissin' on a flat rock," he announced.

Hummer half smiled, still wondering what to do, sitting on the edge of her seat. She wondered how the calf was.

"Feel like going to the auction, do you?"

Her head moved up and down in answer, though it seemed to Hummer that it really wasn't a question. She'd never been to an auction. She wondered if she shouldn't ask her dad first or something, but Riley already had the engine cranking over.

She set her books on the seat between them.

Something in the starter caught and rattled, and Riley muttered under his breath. The truck finally started and he palmed the gear lever, switching on the windshield wipers as the pickup rolled backward out of the driveway.

"Your dad's taking care of your chores tonight," Riley said. "He buried the calf for you too. Said to tell you."

Hummer looked up and felt her throat go tight, but didn't try to speak over the rattling of the pickup. Several times they hit ruts that jolted Hummer out of her seat. She grabbed the seat edge and braced her leg against the door.

"Hang on," Riley told her, raising his voice above the racket. "She ain't much of an easy rider. The shocks are about done for."

Hummer didn't answer. She couldn't help but cry for just a moment, wondering if her dad had put straw in the hole around the calf's body. The road went from gravel to pavement with a bump, and the truck quieted down. Finally Hummer dried her eyes.

SIX

Just as Hummer thought that Riley had forgotten about her, he glanced in her direction. "The best horse I ever had," he said, "was a little bay that looked like Roxie. Or Fox, or whatever you call her. A little smaller but had the same top line." Fox had a beautiful top line because of her long neck and straight back. "His name was Hobgoblin. He could do everything but dance a jig. I held the state barrel-racing championship with him for ten years running."

That was a long time, almost as long as Hummer had been alive. She said so, and Riley nodded.

"Between rodeos I used to show him some, but I did it a little different than everyone else. I didn't use a bridle."

Hummer looked up in surprise. "How could you make him go where you wanted him to without a bridle?" she asked.

"With my weight and my legs. And my voice sometimes." He looked at her to see if she understood. "I'd make sure I was the last one into the arena, and then I'd wait just a minute, to make sure I had everybody's attention. Then I'd slip off his bridle and hang it on the gatepost. I'd show him like that."

"Did you win?"

"Sure I did. Every time. Got so sick of blue ribbons I had to start making mistakes on purpose just to get some red ones." He grinned a toothless grin at her, and she smiled back.

"Must have been something to see," she said. "Fox, she'd probably run away. Or get so excited she wouldn't go where I wanted."

"She's a powerful horse," Riley said. "But so was Hobgoblin, and they all got minds of their own. Ain't no easy circus trick." Riley pulled off the highway and pointed. "Lookit there."

Past the slapping windshield wipers, Hummer could see rows of pickups and horse trailers surrounding the auction house. In spite of the rain, there were horses and people everywhere. More than Hummer had ever seen in one place before. She sat back in the seat.

Riley pulled in between a red eight-horse trailer and a van and swung stiffly out of the cab into the drizzle. He opened Hummer's door and held out a gnarled hand to help her down.

"Ever been to a horse auction before?" he asked as he slammed her door and started toward the barns.

"No," she said, following close behind him.

"It's quite something to see if it's your first time."

"Reminds me of a carnival," Hummer said, "with food and all and people." They were passing a barbecue stand. Something smelled good.

He nodded and then jerked his thumb at the barn entrance. "You get outta the rain. I've got to get a bidding number."

She watched him walk away in his hobbling gait, and then the flow of people moving into the barn pulled her along. She wondered what Riley had come to buy.

The barn was warm, too warm for horses, Hummer thought, but it did feel good to her after being wet. The rain's patter on the tin roof sounded louder and more fierce than it really was, and the horses were nervous because of it. She could hear them stamp and snort and circle in their stalls, up and down the aisle. Somewhere, a horse squealed loudly, and the heavy thuds of kicking followed. Hummer was glad Mike and Fox weren't there.

Hummer stopped to watch a pen of colts. There were five of them, and they kept dashing from corner to corner and crashing against each other as people came by. Their eyes were big and rolling.

"Jumpy, aren't they?" a girl beside her suddenly said.

Hummer looked at the red-haired girl, who was leaning against the gate, looking at the colts. "They sure are," Hummer answered.

"Are you buying or selling?" the girl asked.

"Oh, neither. I already have a horse," Hummer told her. Then she realized it would sound strange if she said she had come to the auction with an old man and had no idea why she was there. "I'm just here with my mom and dad. They might buy something. They might buy a horse for my mother if they find one good enough."

"That's my pony there. We're trading him for a horse." The girl pointed to a nervous-looking black pony standing in the center of his stall with his ears pinned back. He kept throwing threatening glances at the horses in the stalls on either side of him. "He's not really mean," she added, "he just doesn't like strange horses around."

"No wonder," Hummer said. "They're bigger than him."

The girl laughed, and Hummer felt pleased.

"What kind of horse do you have?" the girl asked.

"Arabian mare and a Shetland pony. Plus my folks have Arabians. I live on a horse farm really." She couldn't admit that the horse she rode was just borrowed and that she didn't even know how long she could keep her.

"You're lucky," the girl said. "I bet all you have to do is ride."

"Um hmm," Hummer said. "My mom and dad take me to horse shows all summer. They always come with me and watch and take pictures and things."

The girl looked at the colts again and picked at the paint on the board Hummer was sitting on. She didn't say anything.

"Got a whole wall of ribbons," Hummer offered. "Mostly blue ones. I really show a lot; I'll probably be the state champion again this year. Last year I was the state champion, and I won a trophy almost as tall as this." She held her hand at waist level to show how high the trophy stood. "Do you go to horse shows?"

The girl shrugged and shook her head. "The people there are too stuck up," she said, and turned around.

Hummer watched the girl weave her way through the people and thought for an instant of following her to tell her she really had never been to a show, but she didn't. She sighed and wondered if it was true about show people being stuck up and all. Maybe she should have told her that she trained horses instead. Or something.

Riley bumped something against Hummer to get her attention and she jumped. He was carrying a western saddle on each hip, holding them by the pommels. Riley swung one of the saddles toward her and she caught it. The saddle was lightweight, the leather dark and supple. It smelled good.

"What are they for, Riley?" she asked. They were big saddles, but the seat was small and the stirrups short, as though meant for a small person on a big horse. Both were obviously well used.

"They're youth saddles for you to try out," he said. "If you're going to be riding my horse, you better have the right equipment to do it with."

He was heading for the front of the barn and Hummer followed him. "Riley, are you going to let me keep Fox?" she said to his back, trying to keep the excitement from her voice.

He turned and looked at her sharply. "Whose do you think she is, yours or mine?"

Hummer felt her face go hot and she answered quickly. "Yours."

Riley grunted his satisfaction and heavily swung the saddle over a wooden saddle rack. He motioned for Hummer to get on. At least he didn't seem mad at her.

When the bidding finally started, Hummer and Riley were seated at the top of the grandstands, each with a barbecue in one hand and a Styrofoam cup of lemonade in the other. Hummer concentrated on making teeth marks in the cup while she listened to the auctioneer.

"Twennyfiveadollabiddinow, thuttydollathutty, willyagimmethuttybiddinowathuttydollarrrr." The auctioneer rapped his mallet on the counter. "Thuttydollabiddinowfortydollaforty, who'llagimmeforty? Biditupafortydollarrrr."

Another rap. His helpers were holding up a harness, turning it over and demonstrating the strength of its tugs.

"Riley," Hummer said. "How does anybody know how much to pay?"

"Ain't you listening to him?" Riley nodded at the auctioneer. "Gotta listen to him."

"Fortydollabiddinow, fiftymakeitfiftygimmefifty, biditatafiftydollarbillll."

Hummer began to get the hang of it. Every time somebody waved a hand, the auctioneer got to take a breath and start a new call. If nobody waved for a long time, he'd wait until he was out of breath, then yell "Sold!"

When the little dark saddle came up, Riley began to bid and pretty soon the auctioneer shouted "Sold!" again. Riley smiled at Hummer, then went back to bidding. He ended up with a leather halter, a couple of lead ropes, and a saddle blanket, all of which were passed up the grandstand over the heads of the people below. Hummer held the saddle in her lap. She leaned forward on the saddle and closed her eyes so she could concentrate better on what the auctioneer was saying. It was warm in the bleachers. Riley had to nudge Hummer awake when it came time to go.

The horses were just beginning to sell and the grandstands were packed, but the two of them wove their way down the bleachers, and Riley settled the bill. Outside, the rain continued to pour down, and it woke Hummer up to run through it and jump into the truck with her new saddle.

On the way back Hummer had plenty of time to wonder why Riley had bought her the saddle. Just because she needed one didn't mean Riley ought to buy it. After all, he wasn't rich. Hummer snuggled the saddle closer in her lap, thinking that Riley must like her. She had an idea of something she could do to please him.

SEVEN

In the morning after the cows had been milked and turned out, Hummer led Fox into the barn. She pushed closed the sliding door and swung a gate across the entrance to the calf pens. She was humming.

The inside of the barn was huge, big enough for all eighty head of cattle to be in at once, comfortably, and it was clean. Sawdust-bedded cow stalls lined the barn on both sides, and a big flat cement feeder ran lengthwise through the middle of it. The feeder, called a bunker feeder, was half as high as Hummer was tall, and again as wide. Light, wafting in through the skylights, caught bits of dust in the air, a clean, fine dust from silage and wood chips, and it didn't bother anything.

Hummer led Fox to the feeder and then climbed from there to the mare's back. Fox turned her head to look back at Hummer, her eyes dark and warm.

"We're going to try an experiment," Hummer told the mare solemnly. She reached forward, slipped Fox's bridle off, and tossed it onto the feeder. Hummer took a deep breath and clung tightly to Fox's back. Nothing happened. Fox didn't move. In fact, she didn't seem to notice that Hummer didn't have the reins in her hands. She rubbed her lip on the edge of the feeder.

At last Hummer squeezed her lower legs gently and clucked her tongue to get Fox moving. The mare walked randomly down the center of the barn near the bunker feeder, and Hummer wished she had her bridle. She just didn't know how to get Fox to do anything without it. She twisted to gaze at the bridle on the bunker feeder, and in that instant Fox shifted too.

When the mare stopped in front of the feeder where the bridle lay, Hummer took a breath in amazement. She had an idea. She squeezed her legs and stared at the water trough. Fox went toward it. She looked back at the bunker feeder, and the mare turned around and stopped in front of it.

Hummer hugged Fox's neck. "I get it," she said. She picked out one of the cow stalls and aimed Fox toward it. "Wherever I look," she announced, "that's where you go." The mare walked into the stall, stirring up dust. "No," Hummer corrected herself. "Wherever I look, that's where my weight goes, and that's where you go." She laughed. It was simple. Fox already knew the signals because she received them every time Hummer rode her. "This is no different than riding with a bridle," Hummer told Fox, "except, I don't have any reins. Except, I don't need any reins."

54

Hummer thought of her new saddle hanging on a rack in the milkhouse and smiled. Maybe now Riley would see how much she appreciated him.

Hummer and Fox backed out of the stall and jogged across the barn. They made circles and figure eights, lopsided at first but gradually improving as Hummer learned how to shift her weight. They went from a slow trot to a fast trot to a canter, but then Hummer didn't know how to slow her down.

"Whoa," Hummer said. They were heading toward the water trough. She leaned forward and gripped tighter with her knees. "Whoa, Fox." Hummer looked to the left and turned the mare abruptly into a cow stall. Fox had to stop. She lowered her head and blew through her nose, ready for more. Hummer hugged the mare hard around the neck. This was great. She couldn't wait to show Riley. Maybe by the time he came she would have figured out how to stop.

"Coming to the truck stop with me?" Virgil called.

Fox jumped and Hummer looked up. Her dad stood in the parlor door. "Coming with me?" he asked again.

"Okay," Hummer answered. She leapt off Fox's back, hugged her neck, and ran to open the barn doors. She grabbed the bridle off the bunker feeder and gave Fox a quick pat on her way to the front of the barn.

"Why don't you see if your ma wants to come with us," Virgil said to Hummer as she climbed into the truck. "Run," he added. "I'm hungry."

Hummer raced to the house, but she knew Leona

55

wouldn't come. Hummer ran through the kitchen and into the living room. "Ma," she called, and stopped short.

Leona was in the big rocking chair with an old blanket around her shoulders. She was rocking as hard as she could; the joints of the chair creaked and strained with the weight. Leona was sucking her thumb. She did not look up. Hummer turned and ran out again.

"Not coming," she gasped as she jumped into the truck. She stared out the window, gritting her teeth. She wanted to tell her dad how her ma was getting crazy, but somehow the words just wouldn't come out.

Ma's in there sucking her thumb, she imagined herself saying, as if it were, Ma's in there cooking supper, or, She's dusting the living room. But Hummer couldn't do it. Not even to her dad could she say such a thing. Or, she amended, especially to her dad she couldn't say such a thing. After all, Leona was his wife. He didn't want to know. She stared out the window on the way to the restaurant.

Riley's pickup was in the parking lot, and some bicycles leaned against each other in the bike rack. That meant the gang was there. Two gangs really, if you counted the old people drinking coffee at the tables as one and the kids in the back playing video games as another.

A screen door led from the grocery part of the store into the restaurant. Hummer peered through it as she waited for her dad to buy a paper. She recognized most

56

of the people. Riley, for one, and an old couple, Ethel and Harlow Boss. Harlow was twirling his mustache as usual. Hummer wondered how anybody could ever look Harlow in the eye when his mustache was twirling.

Elsie and Ernie Pritchard sat across from Riley. They owned the gravel pit. Junior Van Duinen was the man with the dirty face, the youngest person at the table. He worked in Ernie's gravel pit and always looked as though he had washed in a hurry. Junior sat at the far end.

A stranger was sitting next to Riley. He kept nodding his head, listening to what the old man had to say. Hummer heard Riley mention Fox, but just then Virgil pushed the door open in front of her and motioned for her to go on in.

"There she is now," Riley said. "Little scrawny runt of a thing, but by golly, she rides my horse like she was born to it." He winked at Hummer. "She don't seem so small when she gets on that horse."

"She rides your Arab?" the stranger said.

Riley took a sip of coffee. "She ain't no ordinary kid."

Hummer could feel her ears going hot, and she pretended not to hear.

"Pull up a chair," somebody said, and Elsie moved to shove some pie plates out of the way. Virgil and Hummer took the empty spots next to Junior. A waitress came with coffee, and Virgil ordered their supper.

"The usual," he said, "with a hamburger and fries for squirt, here." The usual meant a hamburger and fries for him, plus two more burgers to take home to Leona. That's what they usually had, unless there was a special on chicken or something. Hummer loved the chicken.

"You two haven't met, have you?" Harlow asked, twirling his mustache and gesturing to the man by Riley.

Virgil shook his head, and the stranger held out his hand.

"Bernard Poll, Waukau's new fire marshal. Moved in right next door to Ernie, here. Nice to meet you."

Hummer heard her dad reply, and both mentioned the weather, but she twisted in her chair to see who was playing video games in the next room. She recognized Mary Lou from her class and a couple of boys. Mary Lou turned to look at Hummer, who looked quickly away, then back again when it was safe.

All the kids who lived near the truck stop turned up at the video games some time during the day. They came in groups of three or four and drank soda pop while they played. Hummer knew she'd never dare go near the video games.

"Want a quarter?" Virgil asked.

"What?" Hummer looked at him.

"Want a quarter for a game?"

Hummer shook her head, thankful the waitress was bringing their hamburgers. "Hungry," she mumbled, then, "thanks." She stared over her shoulder again, between bites, and didn't notice what the people at her table were saying until she heard the word "horse." She turned her head.

It was the fire marshal, talking to Riley. "My wife used to race her horse cross-country too," he was saying, "in one of those competitive trail rides you're talking about. It wasn't a true race, more of a timed thing, and she had to ride forty or sixty or whatever miles within a certain time limit."

"Sixty miles all in one day?" somebody asked.

"Yessir. Those horses are in top condition. Solid muscle and just raring to go. It took her three months to get her horse ready for one of those races."

"Did pretty good, did she?"

"Oh, I think she took a second once. Something like that, it's enough just to say you completed the ride. A lot of horses don't come in under the time limit and always a few don't make it at all."

Hummer looked up. "You mean they die?"

"Oh, no. Not that. They have vets all along the way, making sure nothing goes wrong. If a horse doesn't look so good, he gets disqualified and takes a free ride back to camp."

"Oh." Hummer took the last bite of her hamburger and wondered if Fox could handle something like that. She guessed that she could, if she were conditioned and all. Hummer wanted to try.

Virgil stood up when he finished his third cup of coffee, and nodded goodbye to the regulars. Hummer followed him, carrying the extra bag of hamburgers.

Hummer was still thinking about the competitive trail ride when she went into the house carrying her ma's hamburgers. Her dad headed straight out to the barn to start chores.

"Ma," Hummer called, and listened for an answer. She heard nothing. The rocking chair was empty. "Ma, I've got your supper."

She walked all around the first floor of the house, looking into the rooms. Nothing but a mess. When she opened the door of the den, a stack of something fell from the roll-top desk onto the huge pile of bags on the floor. Almost before it landed she slammed the door shut, her heart beating fast.

"Ma!" Hummer's voice shrilled with a touch of panic.

Now she heard it: a muffled noise from upstairs. She climbed the stairs. A light shone from under the bathroom door.

"Ma? Are you in there?"

The noise stopped. Hummer knocked and then tried the door. It was locked. She could hear the softest crying.

"Let me in, Ma," she said, rattling the door.

The crying got louder. For an instant, Hummer wondered what to do. Then she plunged down the stairs, taking them two and three at a time. She ran as fast as she could to the barn and burst into the milkhouse. Her dad was swinging the long milk pipe from above the sink to the cooler. He looked at her in surprise.

60

"Dad, hurry," she cried, all her words coming out in the same breath. "Ma's locked in the bathroom and something's wrong."

He didn't ask any questions, but dropped the milk line and followed Hummer back to the house at a run.

"Leona?" Virgil called on his way up the stairs. He shook the bathroom door frantically as Hummer had done, and again they could hear the crying. For several moments he did nothing, looking as desperate as Hummer felt.

"It's okay, it's just me," he said finally. "Virgil. Unlock the door."

Leona wailed from inside.

"Honey," Virgil begged, "let me in now. Everything's okay. It's just me. Let me in."

"We just want to help," Hummer said.

Virgil took a jackknife from his pocket and wedged it between the door and the doorjamb. He slid it up and down until he found the right spot and then he pushed hard on the knife to force the door open.

Leona sat on the floor, her back against the wall and her knees hugged to her body. A dirty blanket was around her shoulders and she sobbed into it.

Virgil knelt on the floor in front of Leona and took her hand. "What's wrong?"

"Don't look at me," she cried, hiding her face.

"Why? What's wrong? Now, it's okay. You can let me see you."

Leona looked up and, for an instant, Hummer had a

61

terrible scare. Leona's face was painted red. There was purple and blue smeared heavily above her eyes, and the black of mascara in heavy lines nowhere near her lashes.

"Don't look," Leona cried again.

"What happened?" Virgil asked her.

"I kept putting more on, but it's still too bright," she explained, and broke into sobs. There was a small empty rouge jar in the sink.

Leona sobbed and sniffed so sadly that Hummer started to cry too.

"I'm so lonely," she added, "and nobody cares. You don't care. You leave me all by myself." She pulled her hand away from Virgil.

"Leona, that ain't true. I do so care. You're still here, aren't you? Someone else might have sent you away when the house got so messy, but I want you here."

"I don't want to go away," Leona agreed. She seemed to know where Virgil meant.

"I know," Virgil assured her. "You want to stay right here, and this is where I want you." He took her hand back and grasped it tightly.

"I still get lonely," she said.

"Why, you never want to go anyplace. You won't go to the truck stop to eat or go into town for groceries or anything."

"I wouldn't know what to wear," she explained. "I really couldn't go out. My head aches so. Tell them that, at the truck stop. That's why I can't go." The tears ran down her cheeks, making watery paths through the red rouge.

"Honey, you ain't never got to go out again if you don't want. Now don't cry." He pulled some tissue off the roll by the toilet and wiped the tears from her face.

Hummer found some cold cream and handed it to him.

"You'd be happier without me," Leona said. "I'm just in your way."

"There, there. You are not. You know that's not true." He gently rubbed the cream onto her face with the toilet paper, the red and purple and blue colors coming off in streaks. He moved to throw the dirty tissue into the toilet, but Leona caught his hand.

"We might need that," she said, putting it carefully on the floor. She squinted at it, then moved it slightly. Hummer stood up, as a hint to get going, because she knew Leona could spend hours rearranging the same little thing.

Finally Leona allowed Virgil to help her to her feet and lead her down the stairs.

Hummer and Virgil did the milking late that night. The cows were nervous because of it. Their bags were hard and swollen, and they wouldn't let down all their milk. Hummer pressed her forehead against the cows' flanks as she washed them, massaging their bags with hot water and humming to calm them. She liked the smell of the cows. They smelled sweet and warm, like green hay.

Hummer washed and dried each cow while her dad followed her, putting on the milkers.

"I like it when you come in the house," Hummer said finally. She felt relieved. Virgil was taking care of things now.

He smiled at her, briefly. "Your ma needs a bath," he said.

EIGHT

"If you're going to ride," Riley said the next day, "the one thing you gotta be able to do is fall. Fall off and bounce back on like you never knew it happened." He and Hummer were in the yard by the hitching post.

"Oh, I've fallen off before." Hummer shoved her hands into her jeans pockets and shifted her weight to one foot.

"I know, but Fox ain't no kid's pony. This is a little different."

She nodded.

"I'm going to teach you to fall, and all you gotta do is what I tell you."

Hummer flipped some hair out of her eyes. She started to ask Riley a question and then changed her mind. Maybe she shouldn't say it, but wasn't it a little crazy to learn to fall? Staying on seemed to be the important thing.

"What I want you to do is pretend there's a long string tied around your right ankle."

Hummer looked down at her ankle.

"When I say so, a little dwarf standing over there," Riley pointed to Hummer's left ankle, "is going to pull your legs out from under you, and you'll land on your right side." He spit into the grass behind him. "Understand what you're gonna do?"

"What about the little dwarf?"

"He's going to pull the string tied to your ankle. He's strong as a bull ox. Every time he pulls, down you go." Riley slapped his hands together. "Bam."

Hummer took a good look at the ground beside her. "Okay," she said finally, pulling her hands out of her pockets. She didn't seem to have much choice in the matter.

Hummer held her breath and swallowed and then toppled sideways. For an instant she saw the ground coming up at her. Her stomach lurched, and, before she knew it, she caught herself with an elbow and was on the ground.

"Not that way," Riley said. "You'll break your arm. Think of your body as a wheel. The arm hits last, and the hand slaps the ground. Just relax a little bit." He nodded to the dwarf.

Hummer pretended her legs had been swept out and she fell again. The earth felt softer this time. It was fun. She giggled when she noticed some cows at the fence, staring.

"Better," Riley said. "Not quite so stiff. Pretend you're made of rubber. Rubber won't break, it just bends. Glass breaks, it's got no give at all. Try again."

She did, and then about a dozen more times until Riley was satisfied. By then, all the cows were lined up at the fence, along with both horses. Fox snorted, and Hummer giggled helplessly.

Riley looked from the cows to Hummer and back to the cows again. "Dingier than jingle bells," he muttered. "That's a start," he added, "but don't go and forget it now. Practice on your own until it's automatic. There's no time to think about how you're gonna land when you get thrown from a horse. You just gotta do it."

He headed toward the truck. "Got something to show you," Riley said over his shoulder, and Hummer ran to catch up. "Just wanted to see if you'd be interested in this." Riley reached for a colored paper on the dashboard of the truck. He handed it to Hummer.

Hummer caught her breath with excitement. It was a flyer for a trail ride. It said, "McKinley Horse Association Fifty-Mile Competitive Trail Ride," on the front, with a picture of a horse on it. Inside, it said, "August 30, Rain or Shine, all breeds welcome," followed by a list of rules.

Hummer exclaimed, "Fox could do it. I know she could. We could do it!"

Riley's face wrinkled in pleasure.

"She could, couldn't she?"

"Of course she can. You're gonna spend the summer training her. If your pa says yes, which he might not."

Hummer wanted to run straight to the barn to look at

67

the mare, knowing she could keep her for a while. She wanted to brush her again, and then ride, this time knowing that Fox was practically her own horse.

"You're gonna start her out soft, because she ain't been in shape for three years. Then you'll build her up slow."

"Riley, is this a race?"

"It's a race against yourself. Your own horse racing herself. Every horse has to run the same fifty miles in the same time – no faster, no slower – and the winner is the horse who goes easiest. The critter in the best condition takes the blue ribbon."

"How can they tell?" Hummer asked. "Which one goes easiest, I mean." She thought it would be easier just to see which one crossed the finish line first.

"Vets check them out. Test their heart rate, breathing, see which horse recovers quickest. They can tell, all right."

Just then Virgil's truck pulled into the yard, and Riley gestured toward it. "But that's only if your pa says you can go."

When Virgil's truck door closed with a slam, Hummer turned and waved. He beckoned for her to come.

"Be right back," she said to Riley, and ran across the lawn to her dad.

He gave her a bag of sandwiches, still warm, from the restaurant. "Take these in to your ma," he said. "One is for you."

"Okay. Dad, you should see what Riley's got."

"What's that?"

"A flyer for a trail ride. He says he'll take me to it. If it's all right with you. It's fifty miles, all in one day, and I'm going to train Fox to do it. I have to start out real soft, then work up from there. Can I go?"

"Dunno yet. You take those in to your ma."

Hummer went into the house blinking her eyes to adjust to the lack of light. It was hot inside. She couldn't see how her ma could stand to be in all day. "Supper is here," she yelled. Hummer opened the bag and looked inside. Hamburgers.

Leona shuffled out of the bedroom, her short hair matted and standing up on one side. "Dad brought supper," Hummer told her, suddenly distracted. She looked at her mother, remembering how she used to wear different dresses every day, and smell nice. "Are you all right?" she asked. She wished that Virgil would have come in again.

"I'm hungry," Leona answered.

Hummer took out her own hamburger and handed Leona the bag, with two left in it. "You should come outside. It's nice."

"I couldn't." Leona took the sack to her rocking chair and sat down. Hummer heard the chair creaking as she opened the door, and she turned around.

"Ma?"

Leona was eating fast, with half a hamburger in her mouth and ketchup on her chin.

"Brush your hair, Ma," Hummer said. It came out

69

soft, and Leona didn't hear it over her own chewing.

Outside, Riley was leaning on the hood of his pickup. "Talked to your dad," he said to Hummer. "He says you can go on the ride if you want."

Hummer smiled. Riley could talk her dad into anything. "Thanks," she said, and unwrapped her hamburger. It didn't look appetizing, though. She was remembering Leona's hair.

"What's wrong?" Riley asked. "Change your mind?"

"No!" She squinted up at him. "Riley, I've got something to show you. Do you want to see?"

"Guess I've got a few minutes," he said.

"It's in the barn."

They went in through the milkhouse and Riley leaned against the door. He watched Hummer shoo a few cows from the water trough. "Giddup, bossy," she said, and patted and pushed them out the door at the far end. "Come on, Frita. Out you go."

They went out, and Fox came in. She rubbed her head up and down against Hummer's shoulder and then nuzzled her pocket. "Hi, prettiest of foxes," Hummer said. She gave her a piece of carrot from her pocket and smoothed the mare's forelock down the center of her face.

"I'm coming up," Hummer warned Fox and then slid onto her back from the bunker feeder. Fox shot her head up, shaking her mane. Suddenly nervous, Hummer stroked Fox's neck to calm herself down and then

70

squeezed her legs gently against the mare's sides. Fox began walking.

Hummer didn't look at Riley at first. She rode Fox around the barn, using her weight to shift direction and her legs to speed the mare up. They went from a walk to a trot, making serpentines and figure eights.

When Hummer dared look at Riley, he was smiling and nodding, so Hummer felt a surge of pride. "Riley, I can do it," she called to him from across the barn. "I can do it like you said." She held her arms out and urged Fox into a canter. Then Hummer turned her into a circle to slow her down and swooped the other way. They ran past Riley at a near gallop. When Hummer turned Fox into a cow stall, she slid to a stop, and Hummer flew against her neck, hugging it hard. Dust floated up around them.

Hummer turned to smile at Riley and then gave Fox the last bite of carrot. "See?" she said.

"Don't know how to stop her, do you?"

Hummer shook her head.

"Bring her out here again."

Hummer backed Fox out of the stall.

"Use your weight," Riley said. He crouched as though he were riding a horse and showed her what he meant. "If you had a bridle, you'd pull the reins a little, and what else?"

"I guess I'd lean back?"

"There you go. Lean back and tuck your butt under

71

like you know she's gonna stop. Try it from a walk."

Hummer urged Fox into a walk, then stopped her. It worked. She grinned at Riley and stroked Fox's neck.

"The one thing you gotta do," Riley said, "is be absolutely confident she's gonna do what you signal her to. If you think to yourself, I wonder if she's going to run through that gate and jump in the river, sure enough, you'll get wet. Understand what I'm saying?"

"I guess so. I guess that's why I couldn't stop her, because I thought she'd keep on going."

"That's right." Riley walked up to them and slapped Fox on the neck. "Remember me?" he asked her. She nuzzled his chewing tobacco pocket. He pulled out the tin, opened it, and put a pinch in his hand. Fox took it carefully with her lips, nodded her head up and down, and swallowed.

"Riley!" Hummer wrinkled her nose. "That's gross."

"They used to think it took care of worms," he said.

"Does it?"

"No, but it don't hurt her none, either." He scratched the mare's ears, then turned to go.

Hummer slid off Fox's back. She opened the big doors to the cow pasture, slapped Fox on the rump, then followed Riley back to his truck.

"One more thing," Riley said as he boosted himself into the driver's seat. He shook the trail ride flyer at her so she'd know what he was talking about. "You're gonna need some things. You've got boots don't you? Good cowboy boots?"

72

Hummer nodded and held up a foot. Her boots were slightly gray with wear but had good heels on them, which is what Riley looked at.

"Those oughta be safe enough," he admitted. "Now, this one is important and you'll need it soon as you start training hard: a horse blanket."

"You mean a saddle blanket?"

"No, I mean a big horse blanket, big enough to cover her up when she comes back from a ride wet with sweat. It oughta be made out of cotton and have a surcingle around it to hold it on."

"Could we buy one?"

"Expensive," Riley said. He drew a circle in the dust on the dashboard. "Your ma doesn't sew, does she?"

"Oh, sure," Hummer lied. "She can sew real good." She had to say it. Riley might think there was something wrong with her ma if she didn't.

Riley looked at her.

"That's what she does all the time," Hummer insisted, "besides clean house and stuff." Her stomach felt queasy. She wished Riley hadn't asked.

"You think she could sew up a horse blanket? Wouldn't have to be nothing real fancy, just so it works."

"A blanket should be pretty easy," Hummer said.

"Well, not too hard," Riley admitted. "Something bright would be nice, red or green or something. A bright color looks good against a dark horse."

"Yeah. I think red," Hummer said. "I'll ask her to make it red."

NINE

Hummer didn't mention the blanket to Leona. She considered it once and stood in front of Leona's rocking chair ready to ask the question, but ended up handing Leona her comb instead. How could someone sew if she couldn't even take care of her own hair?

She wished Riley had never brought it up, about her ma sewing. Or that since he had, he wouldn't come around quite so often. Now that she'd lied to him, things seemed different. She didn't like him as well.

But Riley still came every day as usual. One thing he taught her how to do in her new saddle was post to the trot. He shortened the stirrups, explaining to her how to stand up every other stride. Hummer trotted Fox in a circle and tried to do what Riley said. At first it felt strange and she kept missing beats.

"UP down, UP down, UP down," Riley called out in rhythm with Fox's stride. Hummer began to get the hang of it. The push of each stride gave her the momentum to go up, then gravity brought her back down. It was a lot better than bouncing.

Hummer felt some raindrops on her face and then saw lightning in the sky. It thundered and Fox shied sideways. Hummer tried to concentrate on posting, but Fox was suddenly nervous and broke into a canter.

"Control your breathing," Riley said. He didn't seem to have noticed the darkening sky.

Hummer shortened the reins to pull the mare back down. It always made her a little scared when Fox got nervous. She tried to get her rhythm back.

"Bring her in," Riley said. "You gotta learn how to breathe."

Hummer circled Fox to slow her down, then stopped in front of Riley. "I can't get her to settle down," she told him.

"That's what I'm getting at," he said. "Now, when she starts acting up like this, you gotta settle her down by settling yourself down first. Start breathing real deep and steady, from your belly; don't think about anything but that. See what I mean?"

"You mean, if I get scared, then she gets scared, and if she gets scared, then I get really scared, and then she gets really really scared."

"Yup."

"How can she tell whether I'm breathing with my belly or my chest?"

"Dunno," Riley said. "Now get out there and calm her down. Rain ain't nothing to be scared of."

Hummer trotted Fox back out into a circle, posting and breathing deeply. Fox began to pay attention again.

When Virgil appeared beside Riley, he had a big piece of cardboard held over his head like an umbrella, which he shared with the old man. They watched Hummer and Fox making circles, and Hummer watched their piece of cardboard get darker and darker with rain.

Hummer saw a light come on in the house, and then Leona's face appeared in the window. Virgil and Riley looked toward the house, too. Hummer waved at the square of light, but Leona did not wave back.

"Too bad we don't see more of your wife," Riley said.

Virgil didn't answer for a second.

Hummer pulled Fox closer. She wanted to hear.

"She always was a homebody," Virgil said. "But it's getting so she can't stand to come out."

"Why's that?"

"Dunno. Just can't make up her mind to do it. She don't know what to wear, or how to fix her hair. You know how women are: gotta be all done up to be seen. She don't even want me to see her, if she ain't done up."

Fox had stopped, her butt into the rain and her head down. Hummer twisted a piece of the mare's mane in her wet hands as they stood and listened.

"Yup. Always told myself I was gonna marry that gal and make her happy; give her a little family to love up, a place of her own. She was so pretty, always all made up. Then she starts getting frustrated about things, mad at me every time I turn around. Dunno what I done to make her mad, so I just stay out and let her have her way."

"Maybe what she needs is some pampering," Riley suggested. "New perfume, or things that women like. Maybe she'd take an interest again."

"That's what I do, is pamper her," Virgil said. "Let her have her way. Seems to be working." He gestured toward the milkhouse. "I gotta finish up in there." He left Riley with the limp piece of cardboard.

Riley didn't say anything for a minute, and Hummer stared after her dad. He was finished in the milkhouse, she knew.

"You know," Riley said at last, "if your ma don't want to make that horse blanket, we'll come up with something for the mare."

Hummer's chest tightened and then she said quickly, "Oh, no. She wants to. She's all right, really, and she loves to sew. The reason it's taking so long is just that she's making it real fancy. You know, white trim and embroidery and all. That's partly why she doesn't come outside anymore, she's so busy –"

"Do you know where the Old Durkey Place is?" Riley interrupted.

Hummer nodded, glad for the change of subject.

"You gotta start putting some miles on that mare, getting her out on the trail. Might as well meet you out there, tomorrow morning."

Hummer nodded.

"I'll be there about ten," Riley said, heading toward his pickup. "You get there when you can."

"Sure. That'd be good."

Riley pulled out of the driveway, windshield wipers slapping, and Hummer led Fox into the barn. The mare was soaked, so Hummer rubbed her down with burlap, standing her brown-black hair up in circles all over her body. "Did you ever hear Dad talk like that before?" she asked Fox. Fox pushed her neck into the burlap and stretched out her upper lip. "I never did." Hummer had never thought about her mother as being young or pretty. She wiped the mare's coat down smooth again before she went to help finish cleaning the parlor.

Virgil stood in the pit, washing off the milkers. Hummer took a long-handled shovel and began scraping grain and manure from the floor where the cows had been.

"Dad?"

Virgil stopped the hose and looked up.

"I told Riley that Ma would make me a horse blanket for Fox." She gave the shovel a push. "A pretty red one."

"What did you go and do that for?"

"I couldn't help it. He would've thought that Ma couldn't sew if I didn't tell him she'd do it."

"But she can't sew."

"I told him I'd have it by this weekend."

"Hummer." Virgil switched on a pump to drain milk from the holding tank. It was noisy, so Hummer scraped under the feeders until he switched it off again. He looked up at her. "What am I going to do with you?"

"Can we buy one and tell Riley Ma made it?"

Virgil sighed. "You've got to have one?"

She nodded. "Riley says when Fox gets sweaty, she needs it so she won't cool off too quick and get sick."

Virgil rinsed off the last milker, dried his hands, and then tugged a wallet from his breast pocket. "Then you better have one." He removed some bills and pressed them into Hummer's hand.

"You give this to Riley and have him help you find something." He smiled at her.

"Thank you." Hummer folded the money into her pocket. She stepped down into the pit and began uncoiling the big pressure hose.

"Dad?"

"Yeah?"

"Then Riley will know."

"Know what?"

"That Ma can't sew." She looked down.

"Hummer, Riley don't care one way or the other about that." Virgil started to leave.

"Dad?"

He stopped in the doorway. "Yeah?"

"Did Ma really used to be pretty?"

Virgil frowned and she realized she had said the wrong thing.

"Pretty then and pretty now."

Hummer nodded quickly and Virgil left. She knew Leona used to be clean and smile more. She remembered how Leona used to sing "Lavender's Blue" even long after Hummer had outgrown nursery rhymes, and the face she suddenly envisioned was pretty. She wished she had remembered in time to tell Virgil that.

Hummer aimed the hose nozzle at the floor, then turned on the faucet and the pump. The hose was pressurized and she knew if she ever let go, it would go flying backward out of her hands. She didn't let go. Bits of grain and cow manure went swirling into the drain.

TEN

Halfway between the Ensing farm and Riley's place, a two-track ran off the county road and into the tree line. Hummer and Fox cantered along it, slowly and rhythmically, toward the Old Durkey Place. Hummer sank into the saddle, wondering what to tell Riley about the blanket. She'd promised it would be done today. Her stomach went cold trying to think what to do.

The Old Durkey Place lay about a quarter mile back in a small clearing. People used it some, but it wouldn't be at all busy until fall when the plums ripened. There were a couple of fire pits filled with charred wood and broken glass by the old house foundation, but the lilac bushes were in bloom, so everything smelled wonderful. It was about three miles from the Ensing farm.

When Hummer used to ride Mike there, she liked to eat lunch by the old well. A long-handled dipper still hung on the pump. She thought it was the best water in the world. Or maybe the copper mouth of the dipper made it taste so good.

Hummer stood in the stirrups and patted the mare's neck with both hands, then slowed her to a walk. She could see the clearing ahead and smell the lilacs already. Her stomach fluttered again.

There was Riley's pickup. Riley sat on the old stone foundation of the silo. When he looked up, she waved to him, then stopped at the well and swung a leg over the front of the saddle to slide off.

Hummer looped the reins around her wrist and used both hands and her weight to pull the stiff pump handle down before letting it swing her up to her feet again. She pumped until the water finally gurgled up from the long pipe, then filled the dipper.

She drank until her mouth was too cold to take another drop, stalling for time, and when Fox nickered and nuzzled her, she offered the mare a drink. Curious, Fox snorted into the dipper, spraying the water at Hummer. Riley's laughter floated across the clearing.

Hummer would have taken Riley a drink, but the dipper was attached to the pump with a rope. She led Fox over to him instead.

He stood up, rubbing his knuckles on the mare's neck. "Find the place okay?" he asked.

Hummer nodded. She was here, wasn't she?

Riley didn't ask her if the blanket was done. Instead, he motioned her to the truck.

Hummer slipped a hand into Fox's mane and walked alongside the mare behind Riley. Her hand was trembling.

82

The truck door opened with a creak, and Riley took a big paper bag from the seat. He put the package into Hummer's arms, taking the reins from her. "Open it," he said.

The old man looked pleased with himself, and Hummer wondered what to do. How could she accept a gift when she hadn't kept up her part of the deal? She wished she had never opened her big mouth in the first place. Or that her mother knew how to sew. She could sew if she wanted to, Hummer thought fiercely.

"Go ahead," Riley said. "Open it."

Hummer didn't have any choice. She ripped at the staples, then pulled out a wide, red, folded something. Her throat went tight, first as though she were going to cry, then because she was furious. It was a horse blanket.

"It'll look good on her, won't it?" Riley said. "It's size seventy-four."

"Riley," Hummer said. "Ma was going to take me shopping tomorrow. We were going to make a trip into town to buy the horse blanket, tomorrow!"

"Hummer –"

She talked faster. "Ma had to quit sewing it because her sewing machine broke. She had the material all cut and everything, and then the machine broke."

"Hummer –"

"Ma's going to buy me some other things, too. Another saddle pad, maybe, and some brushes, when we get to the tack store. And new –"

"Hummer!" Riley's voice was sharp.

Hummer caught her breath in her throat.

"That ain't the truth."

Hummer opened her mouth but no sound came out. She was sweating and cold. She felt Riley's voice go gentle before she heard it.

"Your mother can't take you shopping."

Hummer stared up at Riley. She grabbed the reins and swung onto Fox's back, glaring at him. How dare he say that? Her head throbbed and her eyes glazed with tears. He knew about her mother. Not just what Virgil told him, probably, but *all* about her. Hummer's mouth worked and for a moment no sound came out. Then she screamed, "You old man!"

Spinning Fox roughly around, she booted her in the sides, heading toward the woods. The mare bolted in panic. "Old! Old! Old!" Hummer shouted, tears streaming down her face.

A branch whipped Hummer's cheek, and she ducked her head to avoid another. She had to jerk her leg out of the way just in time to avoid having it smashed against a tree. "Fox, whoa!" she screamed.

The mare burst forward again, and Hummer desperately grabbed the saddle horn. She tried to pull the reins, but instead she got a handful of coarse black mane. They were headed toward the road. Hummer could hear the sound of a car.

"Whoa!" she screamed.

When she saw the fallen tree, Hummer felt Fox

gather herself for the leap too late. Fox was already in the air, and she felt herself slipping. "Pretend you're made of rubber," she remembered Riley saying, and then the earth tilted crazily. Hummer slammed into it. She couldn't breathe. She wondered if she were dead and then tried to yell for Fox to come back. There was no air in her lungs. Finally, her breath came back in huge gulps. "Fox," she called. She moved her hands and her arms and then sat up. She was okay.

The tires of a car screeched on the road and a horn honked. Hummer was on her feet and running toward the sound. Had Fox been hit? She tripped once, caught herself with her hands, and then stumbled down the bank to the pavement.

An old dirty blue Duster was backing out of the soft sand in the shoulder of the road. Hummer could hear the clatter of Fox's hooves on the asphalt and she looked just in time to see Fox's tail disappear around the curve. She was galloping along the yellow line on the road.

"Hop in."

Hummer saw Junior's dusty face in the car window. He pushed the passenger door open and she slid in. Junior didn't have to be told to follow the horse.

"Got away from ya, huh?" Junior said as he rounded the bend. Fox came into view again. "Darn near hit her."

Hummer nodded but couldn't stop crying. She didn't even care if Junior saw. Fox was running as hard as she could, terrified, and a car could come from the other direction any minute. Hummer just wanted her back safe in the barn.

"Ain't hurt, are you?" Junior asked.

Hummer shook her head, not taking her eyes off the galloping horse. "Maybe if you put your hazard lights on," she said.

He did so, and drove as closely behind Fox as he dared. There was nothing to do but follow.

"Reckon she's headed home, huh?"

Hummer nodded and glanced at the speedometer. Thirty miles per hour. She wiped her face on her sleeve.

"Fast horse," Junior said.

Don't let any cars come, Hummer thought.

Fox passed the Auroraville store and then rounded the last curve. Hummer could see the silos and then Mike, and she relaxed a little in the seat. No traffic in sight.

The mare turned into the driveway and ran for the barn. The milkhouse door was open.

"Thanks, Junior," Hummer said. She was never going to notice how dirty his face was again. She wiped at her eyes with her sleeve and smiled at him.

"Sure," he said. "Everything going to be okay?"

Hummer nodded and Junior backed out of the driveway. Fox walked out of the milkhouse, eyes rolling. Hummer eased up to the mare and caught the dangling reins. Fox stopped. Her body was wet with sweat and mud and foam, and her veins stood out. Hummer began crying again, softly, while Fox sucked air in great breaths and rested her eyes on Hummer. Already the terror was leaving her, and the white that had fringed her eyes was disappearing.

"Don't trust me," Hummer said at last. "I'm the one that made you scared." Fox kept resting her eyes on Hummer, blowing air, sucking it, not hearing what Hummer said. Finally Hummer took the saddle off, traded the bridle for the halter, and led Fox around the yard until she was cool and dry. Hummer didn't smile at all or pretend the poplar tree was a judge. She knew what she had to do.

ELEVEN

Hummer had never seen Riley's place close up before. At first glance, it wasn't much. Just an ancient shingled cottage and a few twisted crab apple trees. Out back was an outhouse and a horse shed. They were so gray and weather-beaten that Hummer didn't even notice them at first.

Fox nickered to her old home and headed toward the shed, hoping there might be some oats. Hummer pulled the mare back and stroked her neck, then slid off.

A screen door slammed. Hummer looked up to see Riley coming out of the house. He pulled his suspenders over his shoulders and put his cap on his head. Hummer could see by his gray grizzle of beard that he hadn't shaved yet.

Fox nickered again, nostrils quivering.

"Thought my ears were playing tricks on me," Riley said.

Hummer led Fox closer. "Hi, Riley."

"Hi there. What are you doing here? You're up early."
The sun was pink, just over the treetops.

"I'm bringing Fox back."

"Back for what?"

"Back for you."

"What're you talking about? Speak up."

Hummer handed Fox's reins to Riley. "Here," she said. The mare stomped her foot at a fly and looked toward the shed. "I'm bringing her back to you. She's yours, isn't she?"

"Course I ain't gonna take the horse away from you. Why would I do that?" Riley handed the reins back to Hummer so he could pull out his handkerchief and blow his nose.

Hummer stared at her feet. "You gotta take her back. I scared her and made her run away and then she almost got hit by a car and then she ran all the way home from the Old Durkey Place." She looked up at him.

"Well, she ain't hurt is she?"

"No."

"And you ain't hurt?"

"No."

"And she still trusts you? She didn't give you any trouble coming here, did she?"

Hummer shook her head.

"Then what's the problem?"

"I scared her. I mean, she was breathing real hard when I caught her, and she was wet and muddy and stuff." Hummer had to concentrate to keep her throat from going tight when she remembered. "Riley, you just wouldn't believe how scared she was."

"But she calmed right down when she saw you, huh?"

Hummer nodded.

Riley tipped his hat down and sat on the front steps. "When I was training Hobgoblin I wanted to prove that I could train a horse better than anybody else could and that my horse would trust me so much he'd do anything I wanted." He looked at Hummer to see if she understood.

She squinted, wondering what that had to do with giving Fox back.

"So I trained him. I trained him and I trained him, and by Jupiter, that old Hobgoblin woulda jumped right off a cliff if I told him to. Or he woulda swum 'til he drowned. Now that makes you think, don't it?"

Hummer was beginning to understand.

"I ain't that bad a person, you know. Get down on my knees to pray most every night. But I ain't as good a person as Hobgoblin was a horse. Kinda makes you worry when you got a horse who's better than you are, and she thinks you're great, huh? Enough to make you wanna give her away and let somebody else make the mistakes, ain't it?"

Hummer dropped the strand of hair she had been twisting around her finger and stared at Riley. She wanted to say thank you, or touch him or something.

Riley put his hand on Hummer's head. "You keep the horse, little un." Then he turned and gestured toward the shed. "Come on."

"Riley?"

He turned back.

"I'm sorry I lied and I'm sorry I called you old."

"I been called worse."

"Well, I'm sorry."

"It's all right."

Hummer remembered something. "Here's money," she said, taking the crumpled bills out of her pocket. "Dad gave it to me; he said to give it to you for the blanket."

"He didn't have to do that."

"Anyway, here it is." She handed it to him.

They put Fox in the shed and Hummer followed Riley to the house. He held the door for her, and she blinked as her eyes adjusted to the lack of light. She could see three rooms, the big one they were in and two little ones. They seemed spotlessly clean to her.

She didn't realize she'd been holding her breath at first until she noticed how the house smelled lightly of tobacco and leather. She turned to Riley as he stepped inside and let the screen door slam.

"Smells good in here."

"Gonna smell even better when I get some bacon frying," Riley said.

Having shown up at Riley's apparently entitled

Hummer to a huge breakfast. She ate bacon and eggs until she thought she would bust. They didn't talk again until Hummer had slowed down, somewhere around her third helping.

"Never thought such a little runt of a thing like you could eat so much," Riley said.

Hummer smiled and asked for more milk.

"Good thing I had a little food around the house."

Hummer nodded and Riley laughed. "Riley, weren't you mad at me when I ran away with Fox in the woods?"

"I was madder'n a hornet," he said.

"Oh." Hummer looked down at her plate.

"I got over it. That's all. Figured you'd tell me what's going on when you were good and ready." He stood up and picked up their two plates, so Hummer gathered the silverware and glasses.

"There's a bucket hanging out on the pump," Riley said. "Better see about some water for the mare. I'll do this," he gestured at the table.

Outside, Hummer found the bucket, an old metal one, and pumped it full of fresh water. In the stall, Fox took a long drink from it, then set her dripping muzzle on Hummer's shoulder. Hummer smiled, pleased she had given Fox away, so Riley could give her back again.

Riley was sitting in a chair, eyes closed, when Hummer crept by him to use the bathroom. When she came out he spoke without looking up.

"Did I ever tell you about my wife?"

Hummer stared at him. "You had a wife?" She couldn't imagine him being married. He seemed too old.

"Her name was Marguerite. Called her Margo. She was a trick rider."

"A trick rider?"

"Yup. She had a team of palominos, and she'd do her act right after the bronc riding, usually. She had long brown hair, sort of the color of yours. She'd put it up top of her head to do her act, and it never came out. She'd be swinging around, vaulting on and off of those galloping horses, and it never came out."

"What happened? Did she die?"

"Nah. Not that I know of. She run off with one of the bull riders."

"How come?"

"Dunno. Guess she liked him better'n me. Heard he promised her they'd move to Boston and never see another rodeo as long as they lived. Dunno if it's true or not."

"Why? Didn't she like rodeos?"

"She did at first. Guess she just got tired of it. Everybody gets tired of it after a while."

"You didn't Riley. You never got tired of rodeos, did you? I mean, you had Hobgoblin."

"Yup. Guess if I wouldn'ta had him, I'd still have her."

"Which would you rather of had?"

Riley shook his head. "Couldn't tell ya."

The trunk in Riley's bedroom was one of those old kinds with a rounded lid. It was covered with dust. Hummer could see it hadn't been opened in a long time. She sat on it while Riley made the lock work and then jumped off to help him pry the lid up. "What all's in it, Riley?"

"Dunno myself, haven't opened it in so long."

When the lid finally came up, it fell heavily against the wall and the smell of cedar wafted into the room.

"Wow," Hummer said. The trunk was full.

On top Hummer could see folded clothes, and underneath she didn't know what all. Looked like horse equipment all mixed up with shoes, spurs, an old bundle of letters, a lariat, and all kinds of things. "Why'd you keep all this stuff, Riley?"

He moved some of the clothes around, pulled out an engraved beer stein and then put it back. "Just couldn't stand to get rid of it, I guess."

Hummer nodded. "My ma's the same way."

Riley looked up at her. "Got something she won't get rid of?"

"She keeps everything."

Riley found something red at the bottom of the trunk. He pulled it out, then shook it open. Hummer took in her breath. It was the most beautiful blouse she had ever seen. Riley smiled and held it up for her. Silver spangles and red sequins covered the front of the blouse and long silver fringe hung down the back. It had balloon sleeves and tight silvery cuffs.

"Riley, that's beautiful!" she gasped. "Margo must have been really beautiful."

Riley nodded. "You shoulda seen her hair." He slapped at the wrinkles and shook it again, then put it back into the trunk.

Finally he pulled out a picture, black and white and curling up at the corners. "This here's what I was looking for," he said. He turned it to show Hummer.

In the picture, two horses were cantering side by side with a woman balancing straddle-legged on their backs. Hummer could not see the woman's face, but she could see her hair, and the sequined shirt.

"They took this picture for the press," he said. "Had her in the newspaper once."

Hummer smiled at the picture, then Riley returned it to the trunk and closed the lid. "Haven't looked in there for a long time," he said.

"How come you showed me?"

"No reason. Got to thinking about that blanket your ma didn't sew for you. Wondered why she never taught you to sew."

"She really can't sew at all. I was just making that up." She looked up to see if he was angry.

"Why'd you do that?"

"I didn't want you to think she couldn't sew!"

"Aw, I wouldn't care about that. Why would I care?" He scratched his knuckles. "What all kinds of things does she keep, anyway?"

"Everything."

"Ain't never heard of anybody that kept everything."

"Well, she doesn't like to throw anything away. Like newspapers, and ice cream cartons and eggs, even after they've gone bad. Stuff like that."

"What's she want with it all?"

Hummer shrugged. "Guess she's kind of crazy. Dad says she's just going through a stage and she'll get over it, but I think she's a little crazy. You know, she can't sew or nothing. Or cook. She doesn't do things like go shopping or anything, and the house stinks." She swallowed hard.

Riley handed her his handkerchief. "Blow your nose," he said, and then stood up. He went to the door and spit his tobacco, then turned.

"Fox is going to make quite some competitive trail ride horse," he said.

TWELVE

"Ain't having all that garbage around sorta dangerous?" Riley shouted out the window above the noise of the pickup. He was watching the speedometer, trying to stay right at ten miles per hour.

"What do you mean?" Hummer called back. Fox was trotting in long strides with her neck extended, and Hummer stood in her stirrups, weight slightly forward. She kept abreast of Riley's open window.

"The place could burn down faster than Chicago in a dry spell."

Hummer frowned. "Why would it catch on fire? There ain't nothing to set it on fire. Is this still only ten?"

Riley checked his speed a little. "Now it is." He slowed down. "That took six minutes. Comes out right, don't it?"

Hummer figured it out in her head. Going ten miles per hour for one mile would take one tenth of an hour. She divided sixty by ten. "Yup. Six minutes."

Riley handed her a can of spray paint through the window and pointed to a tree. "Right about there," he said.

Hummer rode Fox to the tree, shook the can hard, and then sprayed a blue dot on the bark. This way she could time herself when she rode alone. They were going to mark every mile for about ten miles.

"Rested up pretty good, is she?" Riley asked. "We'll do fifteen miles per hour for the next mile if she feels okay."

Hummer nodded. Fox had been puffing from the fast trot, but already her breathing had slowed. Fifteen miles per hour would mean either a very fast trot or a hand gallop. Hummer gave the paint back to Riley.

"Ready," she said. Fox was chomping the bit, wanting to go again. "How long will it take?"

"I dunno. You figure it out." Riley pressed the clutch down. "Seems like your dad would do something about it."

"Do something about what?" Hummer was trying to divide sixty by fifteen.

"The garbage. Why don't he haul it out?"

Hummer wondered what that had to do with competitive trail riding. Four. Fifteen went into sixty four times. "Four minutes."

"What?"

"It'll take four minutes to do this mile."

Riley put the truck into gear as Hummer pushed Fox forward. She couldn't believe she was actually going to enter a competitive trail ride. Riley said that the speed of the ride wouldn't be determined until the very morning it was to start, depending on the weather, but it would be somewhere between eight and twelve miles per hour. That was fast. At least, if you had to keep it up for fifty miles, it was fast.

Hummer listened to Fox's hoof beats and tried to memorize exactly how fast she was going. Already Hummer had found out that a good fast walk was four miles per hour, and a fast trot between eight and fifteen. Fox could gallop full out at thirty, but Riley said that on a competitive trail ride she should never gallop that fast. It would wear the horse out too much. He said she could practice that fast sometimes, but never do it in actual competition.

Fox's hooves made a steady drumming sound on the dirt road, and the pickup clattered and bounced and jolted along. Fox was breathing hard again, and a sheen of sweat darkened the crease of her neck. Hummer breathed a little hard, too.

"Mile," Riley called out.

Fox slowed to a walk. She drew long breaths of air, and Hummer could feel the mare's rapid heartbeat. She stroked her.

"You count her breaths," Riley said, "and we'll time her."

Hummer turned Fox's head to one side with a rein, and she watched the mare's nostrils fill with each breath. Riley watched his watch for fifteen seconds, and then he multiplied Hummer's number by four.

"Fifty-six breaths per minute," Riley said. He tossed the can of paint to Hummer and watched her catch it against the pommel of the saddle. "Ain't too bad."

Hummer painted the tip of a fence post. August thirtieth seemed like it would never come.

After Fox stood quietly for a few minutes, Riley got out his watch again and they checked the mare's respiration for the second time. She had gone down to thirty breaths for one minute. Riley was pleased.

"Recovery time," he looked at Hummer, "is more important than how high the pulse or respiration gets. She can breathe as hard as she wants when she's running, as long as she recovers real quick once she's stopped." He reached out of the window and took the paint from Hummer. "That's the real test of a fit horse."

Hummer patted Fox's neck. "You did good," she whispered. Fox nickered and stamped. She wanted to go again.

They cantered the next mile, and then trotted, and then hand galloped, and after eight miles Hummer thought Fox was breathing too hard. The mare's nostrils were flared and bright red, and she sucked air in great gulps. Riley got out of the pickup with his watch in his hand. He checked Fox's breathing, then felt under the mare's jaw for her pulse. He finally slapped Fox on the rump. "Ain't nothing to worry about," he said. "She's got space down at the bottom of her lungs she ain't even got to yet."

Hummer felt better. She didn't want Fox to get too tired.

Riley got into the truck again. "We'll walk this one," he said, "and let her catch her breath. You watch. The next time you ride it'll be a little longer before she gets breathing this hard, and the next time longer yet. Ain't nothing to worry about at all."

Hummer thought of something she'd heard once, or read in a book. "Riley, are Arabs really drinkers of the wind?"

The old man spit his tobacco and rolled into first gear. "Sure," he said. "Ever hear how they got that name?"

Hummer shook her head and pushed Fox into a swinging walk next to the truck. Now that they were going so slowly, the truck was quiet.

"Arabs are desert horses. Used to be that the Arab people depended on their horses for everything. Some people even kept their horses in their tents with them. The Arab warriors liked their mares. They wanted mares as battle horses; thought they had more spirit than stallions."

"Fox is spirited, Riley," Hummer said.

"I know it. Mohammed the prophet, he made a test to pick out the best horses in the country. He had the people drive a herd of horses across a desert, then, when they got to the other side, penned them up near a stream. You know how thirsty a horse is after he ain't had no water."

Hummer nodded. Horses need plenty of water; two or three big buckets a day.

"After three days they opened the gate and the horses stampeded for the stream. Do you know what happened then?"

"What?"

"Mohammed blew the battle horn. One long clear blow on that horn, calling the horses back."

Hummer took in her breath.

"Five horses turned back without having had a swallow of water. Not one swallow. And those were the five to father the race." He gestured toward Fox. "Ancestors of hers."

Hummer twirled a strand of Fox's mane between her fingers, thinking she wouldn't want to be the one blowing the horn.

Riley sucked his lips in. "That's how they got to be called drinkers of the wind. After the way they drank wind, instead of water from the stream. Can't you just picture Fox running across the desert sand fast and steady as the wind and sucking air the way she does?"

Hummer could.

When they reached the tenth mile, Riley turned off the ignition and tossed Hummer her lead rope and halter through the truck window. "Time to make some plans," he told her. "Fox can rest a minute."

Hummer tied Fox in the shade and loosened the cinch. She was proud of her for having such ancestors.

Hummer hung her bridle on a tree branch before she climbed into the truck with Riley.

"Sprinting," Riley said. "A couple miles of sprinting a day. That means gallop and hand gallop to get her heart and lungs strong. We want her lungs to work like a big pair of bellows by the day of the ride. Teach her to trot right out. You'll have to work at it, to keep her from breaking to a canter, but it's a better use of energy in the long run. Trotting, she won't tire out so quick. Walking is fine too. But no slow walking. Make her swing them legs out."

"Okay."

"I'll make you a schedule so you know how much to ride. You'll take one day hard, the next day easy. Six miles one day, two the next. Seven miles one day, one the next. Once a week she gets a long ride, fifteen, twenty miles, and then she gets the next day off."

He remembered his tobacco tin, opened it, and tucked some tobacco in his lip. "You know all the timing by now? Six-minute miles for a ten-miles-per-hour trot and all that?"

Hummer nodded.

"Feeling pretty good, is she?" Riley was looking at Fox.

"She doesn't need this rest. Look." Fox was circling back and forth around the tree.

"Well, get out there and get to it then."

She got out of the truck.

"And don't forget to walk the first and last mile."

"Okay."

"You wanna make sure she's good and warmed up. Don't want her pulling any muscles."

"Okay."

Riley started the truck, and then waved from the window. Hummer waved back as she picked her bridle out of the tree.

THIRTEEN

Hummer unfolded the map Riley had given her and followed the blue line with her eyes one more time, even though she already knew it by heart. Trump Lake was fifteen miles away, on the other side of Myrtle Creek, and today she would ride it in an hour. She had kept to the schedule Riley had made a month ago, riding every day for however many miles it said, however fast. The rides were getting faster all the time, and it excited Hummer to think of the map, following it somewhere she'd never been before.

Fox stomped a foot and nudged Hummer out of her daydreaming. The mare's eyes glistened clear and strong. She wanted to get out of the barn and onto the trail.

"I'm hurrying," Hummer said, and began humming as she saddled up. A soft fluffy blanket that Riley had given Hummer went against Fox's back, and on top of that lay the old kitchen rug for extra padding. Hummer walked Fox around and around the yard until she was warm, tightened the cinch, then threw the reins over the mare's neck and swung into the saddle.

The ride was on.

Fox snorted, pushing into the reins until Hummer had let her speed up into a long, ground-covering trot. Once in the woods, Fox traveled with one ear tilted back toward Hummer, the other ear out to the side. They flopped a little when Fox was relaxed, but often they snapped forward, and then Hummer would look for squirrels or other wildlife. Fox knew everything that went on in the woods, and when Hummer was with Fox, she knew everything too.

Hummer could even close her eyes and tell when Fox had something spotted by the way the mare's muscles tensed, or perhaps by the pause in her breathing. If Hummer looked quickly she might see a partridge before it crashed into the air from its hiding place, or catch a white-tailed deer browsing among some tag alders before it went bounding away with its white tail in the air.

The bridge over Myrtle Creek turned out not to be a bridge at all, just two boards lying together across the creek. The planks frightened Fox. She hesitated, backing up and throwing her head. Hummer let Fox stand until she was calm again, then clucked her tongue and Fox stepped onto the boards. She walked straight down the middle, snorting a little and lowering her head, ears forward. The sound of Fox's hooves on the bridge echoed against the water, and Hummer could feel the mare's muscles tense. But then they were across, and Hummer hugged Fox's neck.

They galloped to make up for lost time. Hummer loved the wind in her face and the way Fox flew over the ground. Fox loved to run.

When they burst out onto the dirt crossroads, Fox shied at Riley's pickup parked in the weeds by the path, and Hummer had to pull her around in a circle to get stopped. Hummer never knew where Riley would turn up next.

He was sound asleep.

They trotted up to his open window and Fox put her head through it, nuzzling Riley's tobacco pocket. Riley jumped. Hummer giggled.

"Make it across the creek okay?" Riley asked, squinting, his eyes adjusting to the light.

"Yup," Hummer said. She glanced at her watch to see how long it had taken. "Half an hour so far, and see, she's barely sweating."

Riley nodded, satisfied. "Well, don't wait around here all day," he said, tipping his hat down.

Fox spun around, breaking into a canter, and Hummer had to twist in the saddle to shout "See ya!"

Fox jogged into the woods again. The sun beat down, and Fox was damp with sweat before a glimmer of blue through the trees told Hummer they were nearing the lake. She thought she could smell the wetness of it already. Fox whinnied, thirsty. Hummer pulled her down to a walk. She didn't want Fox to be too hot when she got a drink.

Another quarter mile brought them to a well-used dirt road, and then a grassy boat-loading ramp led them into the water. The mare didn't stop until the water came up to her knees, then she lowered her head and took long drinks. Hummer wished she could get into the cool water too. It sparkled as blue as the sky, and way across it she could see a cabin on the shore.

Fox pawed the water, splashing her belly and Hummer's feet, but Hummer didn't realize what she was up to until she felt the mare's knees begin to fold. "Hey!" she yelled, "Giddup!" just in time to keep Fox from lying down for a refreshing roll.

Hummer turned Fox and they cantered along the shallow edge. Water splashed Hummer's boots and legs and face and she laughed out loud. They trotted and splashed and cantered and splashed until Fox stopped suddenly, ears strained forward. She whinnied a long, trumpeting whinny, and in the silence that followed, an answering nicker floated back to them. Another horse and rider were coming. Fox cantered to the shore, and Hummer saw light bouncing off someone's glasses not far down the trail.

The other horse cantered too, his ears forward and neck strained upward. He appeared white at first, but soon Hummer could see he was speckled with small brown spots – a leopard appaloosa. A girl waved her arm in greeting and Hummer waved back, close enough to see the girl's smile now. Finally the horses stopped, arching their necks in greeting, and trying to snuffle noses.

"Hi," the girl said. "I saw you from across the lake, so I quick saddled up Hawk to come see who it was."

"Hi," Hummer answered. "You live in that cabin?"

"Um hmm. We just moved from Lansing, Illinois. Do you live around here?"

"Sort of around here."

"My name's Charlotte. What's yours?"

"Hummer, and this is Fox."

Charlotte pushed her glasses up on her nose. "This is Tomahawk, only I call him Hawk for short. How old are you?"

"Twelve."

"I knew it; I'm twelve too. And isn't it a coincidence that your horse's name is Fox and mine is Hawk?"

"Um hmm," Hummer agreed enthusiastically. "Both animal names. Hawk is pretty." He was pink around his eyes, and his head was a little long, but he looked strong and proud. Hummer thought Hawk and Charlotte looked alike in a way; they both had freckles.

"Fox is pretty too," Charlotte said. "I love Arabians."

Hummer looked away for a moment, not knowing what to say, but when she looked back Charlotte was still smiling.

"Hey, look." Charlotte pointed to the lake. Some mallard ducks were gliding along the bank. One tipped upside down to pick food off the bottom. "Let's sneak up on them."

Hummer wondered how to sneak on horseback, but she turned Fox to follow Hawk toward the lake. The big gelding did seem to be walking soft on his feet. Hummer thought that his spots probably made good camouflage.

A hen swam out from the bank surrounded by tiny peeping ducklings.

"Oh," Hummer said. "They look soft." She wished she could hold one. She pushed Fox up closer to Hawk, and they took a few more steps before the ducks glided away.

"Too bad they have so many predators," Charlotte said, turning Hawk back to the trail.

"Like what?"

"Turtles, for one thing. They swim under the water and grab the baby ducks by their legs. And foxes. They like ducks."

"Do you have ducks at home?" Hummer asked. She wondered how Charlotte knew so much.

"No, but we're going to have pretty soon, now that we live on the lake, so I've been reading about ducks."

"Oh. Do you read a lot?"

"I read all the time. I'm working my way through the horse section at the library," she said. "Even those big vet books." Charlotte pushed her glasses up. "You must read a lot too, to be such a good rider."

Hummer looked up, surprised. "Oh no. I mean, I hardly ever read. I wouldn't know what to read." She hoped Charlotte wouldn't think she was stupid because she rarely read books. She hadn't meant it to come out that way.

"Really? I have so many books you can borrow. There's this one book called *King of the Wind;* it's about a horse, and if you want I'll bring it along next time we ride together. Do you think you want to borrow it?"

"Sure," Hummer said. She liked how Charlotte had said "next time we ride together."

"Have you had Fox for a long time?" Charlotte asked.

"What seems like ages, but really, only about two months." Hummer swallowed. "She's not exactly mine. I ride her for someone."

"Oh? Who?"

"Riley. He's an old man who can't ride anymore, but he likes to have his own horse."

"Do you go to his house every day to ride?"

"No. I have Fox at my house, and Riley usually comes to watch me. I tell him which direction I'm going to go and he might meet me somewhere in his pickup."

"What are you going to do when Riley takes Fox back?"

"He wouldn't. He really likes me to ride her for him and exercise her and everything. He wouldn't take her back. I don't think."

"Do you ride with your friends all the time?" Charlotte asked.

"Oh. No. I don't have any friends who have horses." Hummer felt a moment of panic.

"Neither do I. You're the first one I've met. I've met two other people since I've been here," Charlotte said. "At a restaurant. Do you know Mary Lou or Troy?"

"Um hmm," Hummer said. "Troy is in fifth grade; he's okay, but Mary Lou is in my class and she's not all that nice. She's my next-door neighbor, only I never see her."

"She was nice to me," Charlotte said.

"Well, I guess she's nice to some people."

"Why? Doesn't she like you?"

"No."

"Well, I like you," Charlotte said.

"Thanks," Hummer said.

Charlotte smiled, then looked at her watch. "What time do you have to be home?"

"Oh, no time really. It doesn't matter."

"Must be nice. I have to be home by lunch and it's ten-thirty now. It's only about half a mile around the lake to where I live though. How far is it for you?"

"Fifteen miles."

"Fifteen *miles?* What time did you leave?"

"About nine. We got here in an hour." Hummer hoped she didn't sound like she was bragging.

"An *hour!*"

"It's all part of the plan," Hummer explained. "See,

112

I'm going to be in a competitive trail ride and I'm getting her ready."

"You are? I've read about competitive trail rides, but I never knew anyone who was actually in one. I never thought anybody our age could be in one. How many miles is it?"

"Fifty. Is it really supposed to be hard?"

"Well, in the books they say plenty of horses don't make it. And you have to work so hard before you ever get there. They say if you miss just three or four days of training you might as well not even go. Aren't you scared?"

"If you knew Riley you'd know it'll be okay," Hummer said. "He worked out the whole schedule with me and everything."

"How long will you be there?" Charlotte asked.

"Just for the weekend. We're going Friday night, spending the night in the campground, and then riding on Saturday."

Charlotte looked almost shy. "Do you think I could come and watch? I wouldn't get in your way or anything, and I could help keep Fox brushed. I read that it helps if you have an extra person to take your water bucket out to meet you on the trail, and stuff like that."

Hummer thought she would burst with excitement. "Could you really come? I'm going to sleep in the horse trailer. It's going to be really fun."

Charlotte bounced exuberantly in her stirrups. "I'll ask. Oh, I just know my parents'd let me, something

113

this important. How far do you have to ride today?" she asked.

"Thirty miles," Hummer said. "Fifteen to get here and fifteen to get back."

Charlotte's face turned serious. "Do you have to ride it all at once? If not, we could take a short break," she suggested. "Otherwise, you know, if we keep on going, you'll have gone more than thirty miles. I brought a halter and lead rope."

Hummer had a rope too, so she nodded. "Good idea."

They picked out a good spot for tying the horses, and Hummer unsaddled Fox, laying the saddle blankets wet side up to dry in the sun.

Hummer and Charlotte sat down cross-legged in the tall grass, talking about what school they'd both be going to—the same one—and telling about their horses. A grasshopper landed on Hummer's cheek and bounded off again. Fox and Hawk stood quietly, noses together.

When Charlotte finally had to leave, Hummer saddled Fox too. Hummer's head buzzed with plans. Next Saturday she and Charlotte were going to ride together again; only two Saturdays after that was the competitive trail ride. She just knew Riley would let Charlotte come along for the weekend.

Hummer couldn't wait to get home so she could ask him. Also, she hadn't had any lunch. She was hungry. She thought she remembered a leftover fish sandwich.

114

FOURTEEN

Hummer woke up shivering. Her sheets were soaked, her hair clung to her temples in damp strands, and chunks of dead fish seemed to be floating in her stomach. She'd once stepped barefooted on a rotten fish and she remembered how its skin sluffed off and the eyes popped out at her. She thought her stomach was full of squiggly black fish eyes.

She reeled to the toilet just in time.

Virgil lay in his cot snoring when Hummer stumbled into the milkhouse. Her arms and legs were covered with goose bumps, but it felt to her as though the milkhouse were a hundred degrees. She leaned against the dewy stainless steel of the milk cooler and vaguely heard her dad saying something.

Virgil took Hummer's hand and led her to his cot, where she sat down dizzily. "Gonna be all right?" she heard him say.

She wasn't sure how to answer. Virgil laid his hand on her forehead. His hand felt cool.

"Got a bellyache?" Virgil asked.

Hummer nodded. Her stomach felt hard and tight, like somebody had been punching it. She held tightly to Virgil's hand as they sat together in the dark.

"What'd you eat last night?"

It made Hummer sick just to think about it. "A gross fish sandwich," she answered. She was never going to eat fish again in her life. Especially not cold fish.

"Where'd you get it? Out of the refrigerator?"

"No. Off the counter." The refrigerator was too awful even to open anymore. She never used it, and anything Leona put in there got left.

Pretty soon Hummer felt so tired she could hardly keep her eyes open. Her head ached and the back of her eyes ached and she longed to lie down. She was shivering again.

"Better get under these covers," Virgil said, and he opened up the sheets for Hummer to crawl into. He brought a bucket from under the milkhouse sink and put it on the cement floor near her head. "You might need that," he added, and sat on the end of the cot.

Hummer pushed her feet into her dad's lap and closed her eyes. She didn't hear Virgil leave, but when Hummer woke up he was gone. The sun shone brightly through the milkhouse window, glaring off the milk cooler, and everything was quiet. She thought she remembered the thub-*dub*, thub-*dub* sound of the milking machine, but now she wasn't sure. She didn't know if it was before or after chores.

116

Hummer remembered that she had to ride Fox and she sat up suddenly. The milkhouse spun in circles and the floor tipped up at her. She sank back down on the cot. Maybe in a few minutes she'd ride. Her eyes closed again.

The next time Hummer woke it was to the sound of voices in the parlor. One of them was Riley's. She smiled, glad he had come. She turned onto her side and opened her eyes. She could hear Virgil clearing his throat, the way he did when he was nervous, and then Riley's voice became louder. "Ain't no place for a kid," he said, and then, "Lucky she didn't get sick a long time before this."

Virgil's voice answered softly, and then Riley was saying, "Just send her away for a week or so; it wouldn't have to be for long. It'd give you time to get the place cleaned up, take care of Leona . . ."

Hummer realized they were arguing about her. Riley wanted Virgil to send her off somewhere. Hummer couldn't believe it. Had he forgotten about the trail ride? She wanted to remind him. She tried calling out his name, but it didn't come out. Hummer tried to keep her eyes open. Her mouth tasted hot and dry, as if it were full of cotton. She let her eyes close.

She didn't wake up again until Virgil sat down on the cot. She edged herself up on her elbows to squint up at him. She felt as if she'd been sleeping for days.

"How you doing?" he asked. "Feeling any better?"

"Um hmm. I'm thirsty." She sat up, and Virgil ran a

cup full of water from the milkhouse sink and brought it to her.

"Thanks," Hummer said, drinking the water slowly, letting it run through her mouth and around her teeth before each swallow. "I had an awful dream," she said. "What time is it?"

"About time to get chores started. We got company coming afterwards."

Hummer realized he was talking about evening chores; that a whole day had gone by while she lay sleeping on the cot. A sinking feeling in her stomach told her she'd never have time to ride that day. Or maybe she could just a little. After all, it wasn't Fox who was sick. All Hummer had to do was stay in the saddle, and she thought she could do that in her sleep.

Just then hot water started running automatically into the deep milkhouse sink, where it would be sucked up into a pipe and run through all the milk lines. Virgil would have to wait for it to complete the cycle before he could start milking.

Hummer looked up. "Company?" They never had company.

"Bernie Poll and I dunno who all else." He twisted the cap on his head. "A social worker or somebody. You feeling a lot better?"

"Um hmm," Hummer said, suddenly cold. "What are they coming here for?" She knew that Bernie Poll was the fire marshal.

"Gonna take a look at the house." Virgil twisted his cap again.

"Inside the house?"

He nodded.

So Hummer hadn't merely been dreaming. Riley had been serious about sending her away. She remembered the time he kept asking her questions about the garbage, and how he said the house must be a firetrap. She groaned.

"Riley's mad that you got sick; he says it's my fault, and he got a hold of Bernie, and Bernie called some social worker, and they're coming out here to see if it's a fit place for you to live." Virgil slouched down on the cot, flopping his head into his hands.

Hummer stared at the cooler. "What if it ain't fit?"

"Foster home for you until it's clean." He didn't look up at her.

So it was true. Hummer couldn't think of a thing to say. She just listened as the hot water completed its cycle through the pipes and then poured out into the drain. Finally Virgil got up to swing the pipeline from the sink to the cooler. "Chores gotta be done," he said. He looked sick himself, pale and anxious.

Hummer stood up too, still in her nightgown. She felt heavy, like her feet were lead. "I better get dressed," she told her dad, and he nodded, following her to the milkhouse door and watching as she walked to the house.

She dressed, trying frantically to think of a way to

119

make the house look better. If only she could get even the kitchen clean, and shut the big living room doors, they'd never know about the mess. She wondered how clean it had to be to be a fit place to live. They probably wouldn't mind a few dirty dishes, as long as the garbage wasn't all over the floor.

Hummer's head throbbed as she ran down the stairs and into the kitchen. Leona was asleep in the rocking chair. Hummer didn't know where to start. The living room doors wouldn't close because so much was stacked against them, and she thought if she took the time to move that stuff there would never be enough time to work on the kitchen.

She opened the oven, but it was already full of dirty pots and pans. The sink was full of dirty dishes, the cupboards were full of dirty dishes, and the counters were piled high.

She decided to take some of the garbage outside and hide it behind the house, but when she lifted the first bag, the bottom fell out, spilling fuzzy green cans and coffee grounds onto the floor. She picked up another bag, glanced into the living room at Leona, and carried the bag outside. Leona would get mad if she knew, but Hummer didn't care. She felt hot and tired, but made another trip, carrying two bags at once. She just had to make the place look fit.

Eventually the table did look a lot better. Hummer washed the front of the refrigerator and the front of the stove. A kitchen chair was free now, so she sat down on it, leaning her face against its back. Her head hurt. She thought of one last thing to do and ran to the bathroom for a hairbrush. Her stomach felt sick again, but this time it didn't have to do with anything she'd eaten. People were going to come in the house. They'd see Leona, and maybe laugh at her.

"Ma?" Hummer shook Leona's arm gently.

Leona stretched and yawned.

"Wake up. Let me fix your hair."

Leona looked at the brush in Hummer's hand and smiled. "Okay, dolly," she said agreeably. She sat up straighter.

Hummer brushed Leona's hair gently, working out the frizzy tangles. Finally she parted Leona's hair neatly down the center. "There," she said. She touched Leona's hand. "Some people are coming," she told her.

"Well, I couldn't go out, not tonight. Tell your dad that."

"They're coming in the house."

"No, they wouldn't come in the house; they're not invited," Leona answered, unperturbed.

"Well, they're coming in anyway." She looked at Leona, feeling helpless. There wasn't anything more to say. Finally she squeezed Leona's hand again and headed for the barn.

When Bernie Poll's station wagon pulled into the driveway, Hummer was on Fox in the yard. The mare arched her neck, head up and ears forward. A red-haired woman emerged from the passenger side door.

The wind blew the woman's feathery short hair into her face, and without bothering to brush it away, she looked up at Hummer and Fox just as solemnly as they looked at her. "Quite a pair you two make," she said at last, and then smiled a beautiful, upside-down, squinty-eyed smile.

Bernie Poll smiled at Hummer too, and then said, "Hello, where's your pa?"

Hummer pointed to the milkhouse just as Virgil appeared in the open door. Hummer didn't smile at any of them.

Mr. Poll introduced the woman as "Yvonne, from the County Department," and before he could say any more, Virgil told Hummer, "Better put the horse away and feed the calves." He was twisting his cap around and around on his head.

Hummer and Fox cantered past the barn, and Hummer slipped off to let Fox through the pasture gate. "I'll be back," she told Fox, swinging the gate shut.

Hummer fed the calves, and for the first time all summer, when she got to the last bottle of milk she couldn't remember which calf was left. They all looked hungry, butting their heads into her. She looked at their noses. She always fed the speckle-nosed calves first, but now she wasn't sure if she had done them all or not. Could the white, speckly-nosed heifer be the one? She sighed and scratched their heads. "I'm sorry," she told them. She knew it was better to let one calf go hungry than it was to make another one sick by feeding it twice. As she washed out the bottles, Hummer realized that her hands were shaking, and she didn't know if it was from being sick, or because those people had come to look in the house. She shoved her hands into her jeans pockets as she walked into the yard. Virgil, Yvonne, and Bernie Poll were gathered around the hood of the station wagon, with Virgil looking at some papers that Yvonne was showing him.

"I know this isn't going to be pleasant for anybody," Bernie was saying, "but the quicker we move, the quicker everything will be back to normal."

Hummer wondered what he meant by move. She didn't know what was going to happen. At least she'd gotten some of the garbage out of the kitchen.

"Old Riley could take her," Virgil said, as if he hadn't heard Bernie, as though he already knew he had lost, but was dickering over conditions.

"You realize it has to be an approved family," Yvonne said. "And in most situations, we feel it's better to get the child away from their own hometown."

"Well, let's take a look," Bernie said finally, and he headed for the house. Yvonne walked beside him, Virgil behind. Virgil's shoulders were slumped and his feet scuffed up dust. Yvonne turned once to smile encouragingly at Hummer, but Hummer couldn't smile back. She just followed them miserably onto the porch.

Bernie's face stiffened as he opened the inner door,

and Yvonne touched her hand to her mouth. Virgil watched their faces for a moment, then quickly brushed past Hummer and out the porch door again. Hummer was left to show them in.

The kitchen didn't look as good as Hummer had thought it did, and the open doors to the living room made everything worse. Yvonne and Bernie looked at each other.

Hummer's face felt burning hot. She stared at the filth of the sink and counter, the dishes all piled together, and the broken sugar bowl half full. Bernie and Yvonne didn't even turn as they stared, or bother to look into the living room. Yvonne looked sick. The coffee grounds Hummer had tried to sweep under the stove were showing. She began crying softly.

Hummer, Bernie, and Yvonne all jumped at the sound of a high-pitched scream.

Leona stood in the doorway of the living room. She screamed again. It was a horrible sound, long and high and angry. She didn't move or say anything, she just stood in the doorway and screamed. Yvonne turned for the porch and Bernie followed. Hummer ran past her mother and up the stairs. She ran into her room and flopped onto the bed, shaking and sobbing. Leona continued to scream downstairs, and Hummer lay curled up, holding her stomach and gasping for breath. It was the worst day of her life.

FIFTEEN

Jack and Florence Pelton arrived in a shiny Buick to pick up Hummer. It turned into the driveway with a crunch of tires on gravel. Hummer saw the glare of their windshield flit across her bedroom ceiling. She had just finished packing. She went to the window and watched as Florence got out of the car.

Florence had short dark hair and a smile that tipped up the edges of her mouth, but Hummer didn't care. When she knocked on the door downstairs, Hummer swallowed and didn't move. The knocking went on until at last Virgil called from the door of the milkhouse.

Hummer watched the woman come back out from under the eaves. Then, carrying her bag of clothes, Hummer crept downstairs past Leona to the back door. She looked back at her mother. Leona, who hadn't spoken since yesterday when the social worker had come, didn't say a thing.

"Bye," Hummer said softly.

Leona rocked in the chair.

The horses were grazing by the fence. They lifted their heads for a moment as Hummer came out, then flicked their tails and went back to their grass.

"I'm leaving," Hummer told them. "Aren't you going to say goodbye?"

Fox swished her tail.

"You don't even care," Hummer whispered fiercely at them. "People are here to take me away and nobody even cares."

Fox swung her head around to bite at a fly, leaving green saliva on her flank. She didn't look at Hummer.

"Hummmmerr!" It was her dad calling from the barn.

Hummer glanced toward the barn and back to the horses. "Bye," she said finally, and when they still didn't look up, Hummer walked toward the barn.

"You must be Hummer," Jack said.

Hummer nodded. She knew their names because Yvonne had told her over the phone that morning. She had to stay with them for one week.

Jack was tall and broad-shouldered, his wife only slightly shorter. Both wore knee-length shorts and sandals.

Hummer stared at Florence's wedding ring, and then at Jack's steady hand held out to take her bag. Hummer relinquished it uneasily.

"Nice meeting you, Virgil," Florence said, then turned to Hummer expectantly. "All set?"

Hummer looked helplessly at her dad as they moved toward the car. "Dad, I don't want to go," she whispered frantically.

Virgil lifted his cap, then resituated it on his forehead. "Reckon you'll be okay," he said at last. "Be good." He gave her a very tight hug, and Hummer hugged back as hard as she could. She thought he was going to cry.

Jack held the door as Hummer slid into the back seat. He handed her the bag of clothes, which she held in her lap. The car rolled out of the driveway and headed north.

Hummer craned her neck and looked out the back window, trying to get a last glimpse of Fox, but when she saw Virgil instead, she was sorry she'd done it. He was leaning back against the barn. Her throat went tight. She wiped impatiently at her eyes, afraid the Peltons would see.

"Hummer, have you ever been to Green Bay?" Jack asked, glancing back.

Hummer shook her head, afraid of what her voice would sound like if she spoke. She did not want to talk to strangers just now.

"We've lived there about five years," he said. "I think you'll like it."

When she only nodded, Florence twisted back. "Let's see, you don't have any brothers or sisters, right?" she asked.

"No," Hummer said.

"Well, what about pets? Yvonne talked as though you had a horse."

This time Hummer nodded her head. "That was her, back there in the pasture, eating."

"What kind of horse is she?"

"Arabian," Hummer said. She missed her already.

"Arabians." Florence nodded. "They're beautiful. We have a daughter who always wanted to have a horse. She loved horses. At the fair, she always had to ride the ponies. Oh, she collected horse statues and horse stamps. Covered her walls with horse posters."

"Um hmm," Hummer said politely.

"Well, Jenny would have envied you, having the actual thing."

"Will she be there when we get there?" Hummer asked, hoping there wouldn't be any more people to meet.

Florence smiled. "Heavens. Jenny's got daughters of her own now. She lives in Florida."

"Oh."

"She comes to visit twice a year, and we spend every other winter down near them. One winter with one daughter, the next winter with the next. Emily lives in Massachusetts. Emily didn't care much for horses; she was more interested in boys. She had posters of rock stars on her wall. But she would have envied you too, growing up on a farm like that. Both girls just loved the country. Have you lived on the farm all your life?"

Hummer nodded again.

"Do you like cows, too? Cows and horses?"

"Um hmm."

"Well, so did Jenny. That's quite something, how girls like their animals." Florence turned around then, as though her neck had a crick in it from being turned so far.

When it looked as though Florence wasn't going to turn back around, Hummer lay her head against the vibrating window. She thought about her dad, leaning against the barn. He didn't want her to leave, but he couldn't do anything about it. People just came and took her. It was the law.

Hummer didn't realize she'd been asleep until she woke with a jerk as the car slowed down. She opened her eyes and saw a small gas station next to a lumberyard. HOWARD CITY, the building said. She'd never heard of Howard City. Hummer thought that Green Bay must be a long way from Auroraville.

The next time Hummer woke up, Jack looked into the rearview mirror. "Almost there," he said. "This is Green Bay."

Hummer felt rather overawed, especially when they drove over a high overpass with two layers of traffic underneath. There were buildings in every direction, and as far as she could see, nothing but miniature streets and houses until, in the distance, they seemed to disappear over the edge of the earth. It was as if Auroraville didn't exist, nor her dad's farm with its silos and poplar trees.

Finally, Jack turned the big car onto a narrower street called Dennison Court and announced, "This is it. We're here."

Hummer felt her heart drop. "Here," far away from home, far away from pastures and woods and cows. She hadn't realized she would miss the cows.

Jack pulled into the driveway and the garage door began opening. Even in the garage, Hummer could smell something good cooking.

Inside the house, the first thing Hummer noticed was all the light. Then she saw where it came from. In the ceiling above the stairwell was a perfectly round yellow-and-blue stained glass window. When he saw her looking up at it, Jack stopped too. "Do you like that?" he asked.

"It's pretty," Hummer said.

"I put that in myself. I bought it from a church in Mexico. Can you see where it was broken?"

Hummer could, once she looked closer.

"They were going to throw it away because it was broken, so I bought it. I carried it all the way back with me."

"Did you fly?" Hummer asked.

"No, I took a bus." He smiled at her and headed down the hall with her bag, so Hummer quickly followed. As she turned into the bedroom behind him, he asked, "Hungry?"

Hummer nodded, suddenly aware that she was indeed hungry, and that she hadn't had anything substantial to eat since she'd been sick.

"Florence has a roast in the Crockpot. Dinner shouldn't be more than ten minutes or so. You could take care of your things, if you want."

Hummer sat on the edge of the bed and looked around. She found that the drawers of the tall dresser were empty and started to put her clothes away, but then took them back out and returned them to the bag. It seemed too permanent to have her things in a dresser. She found her comb and jerked it through her hair, but then there was nothing else to do, so Hummer sat back down on her bed, trying not to make wrinkles in the bedspread.

She felt like she was in the wrong place, like she had been pulled away from her own life. The Peltons seemed nice, but she wanted to get back to Fox and Virgil, and call Charlotte on the telephone. She wanted to see Leona, too.

After supper, Florence disappeared into the study to take a phone call. Hummer sat in the living room looking at an old picture book of horses, which Jack had found for her. She turned the pages, feeling more and more lonely. Finally Florence returned and sat down next to her on the couch. "I've just had a talk with Yvonne," she began. "You know I know all about your mother?"

"Oh," Hummer answered, studying the back of her

hands. She didn't like having people know so much about her, especially so much bad stuff.

"Yvonne says she's a real nice woman."

Hummer looked up.

"She says she went with them, no problem, after the first few minutes. She was ready to go. She knew she needed help."

"Where to?" Hummer asked.

"A nice place not that far from Waukau. It's called Oak Rest. Yvonne says she's taking it real well. She says your dad's more upset than your mom."

"Oh?" Hummer looked up again. She felt bad about him, all alone.

"But he's okay. Don't you worry. He's doing fine too, just like you are." Florence touched Hummer's hand. "It'll all work out for the best," she assured her. When Hummer didn't know what to say, Florence asked, "About ready for bed? You must be tired."

Later, in bed, Hummer wondered what "taking it well" meant. Did it mean simply that Leona wasn't screaming anymore, or that she liked the new place and was happy she'd gone? Was she homesick, like Hummer was?

Hummer stayed homesick all week. In the city, it was hard to get used to having nothing to do. Florence took her to the library for an armload of books, but Hummer found she couldn't concentrate enough to read them. They just made her think about Charlotte.

And she couldn't help wondering, over and over,

about Leona. She remembered Leona crying in the bathroom, how sad she had been, but then that Leona had kept Virgil from throwing away tissue only minutes later. It was as though one moment Leona wanted help, and the next she didn't.

Hummer thought about Riley and how he had betrayed her. Now there would be no trail ride. She remembered yelling at him, "Old! Old! Old!" and then apologizing later. Now she felt madder than ever at him, but, at the same time, she was afraid to be mad. Fox's serene eye stayed in the back of the picture, as though it were the anchor to the jumble of colors washing through Hummer's mind.

On Saturday, Hummer woke with the thought that she was forgetting something. It seemed silly, because what could she possibly have to forget? She didn't have any chores to do and she didn't know anybody here.

At lunch she remembered. With an orange half peeled, Hummer suddenly recalled her plans to meet Charlotte that day. Charlotte and Hawk would be almost around the lake by now. She jumped up from the chair, knocking it backward but catching it before it fell over. "Oh no!" she exclaimed.

Florence jumped up too. "What's wrong?" she asked. "Are you okay?"

Hummer slumped back into the chair. "I forgot. I was going to meet my friend Charlotte at the lake today, but I forgot to tell her I couldn't come. She's going to think I don't like her now."

"Why, I'm sure she wouldn't think that," Florence answered, somewhat relieved. "You can give her a call, and let her know where you are after lunch."

Hummer sat down just in time for the phone to ring. Florence answered it and then called out to Hummer. "Your dad," she said.

Hummer dashed for the receiver. "Dad!"

"Hi, Hummer. Hi, sweetheart. How are you?"

"Okay, but I miss you. How are you? How's Fox?"

"I'm okay. Fox is fine. Far as I know."

"Is she eating good?" Something had to be really wrong to make Fox go off her feed.

"Riley didn't say anything about anything being wrong, but, say, Hummer –"

"You mean Riley's watching her?" Hummer felt suddenly cold.

"Well, sure. He's got her back at his place. Say, Hummer, I'm fixing your room up, just for you. You've got a new rug – it's pink – and we're going to get your walls painted up. You ought to like it real well."

Riley had taken Fox away. No more Fox.

"Right?" Virgil asked when Hummer hadn't said a word.

"Right, sure."

"I miss you around here," he said. "Mike and the calves miss you."

"I miss you, too."

"Your ma's at Oak Rest. I guess you know that."

"Um hmm. How is she?"

"Well, she's clean." Virgil hesitated. "She's doing fine, they keep saying, but she don't have a lot to say. She's quiet. The Peltons are going to take you there for a visit."

"How come I can't go with you, instead?" She was supposed to be at the Peltons only for another two days. Until Monday.

"You and I'll go later. After this time."

"Yeah, okay. Dad?" Hummer was suddenly scared to ask.

"Yeah?"

"When can I come home?"

"That's what I was just getting to. Things are going awful slow. Ernie is helping me clean the place up, hauling things to the dump. But the place isn't ready yet. It's not fit yet," he added. "They have to judge when it's fit, and it ain't yet."

"Oh."

"I'm hurrying, baby, but you'll be all right at the Peltons' for another week, won't you? Look, there's forty dollars in the mail, and when you get it, they're gonna take you shopping."

"Another week?"

"That's not long. It'll go by fast. With shopping to do and all. You could get new jeans to ride in."

Hummer wondered what she'd need new jeans for if she didn't have Fox anymore. Maybe her last ride with Fox had been that Saturday with Charlotte before everything went wrong. She might never see either Fox or Charlotte again. Suddenly she didn't even dare call Charlotte.

"You there?"

"Um hmm."

"I said you could get new jeans."

"Thanks, Dad. That'll be nice."

"Okeydokey," Virgil said. "Be a good girl."

"Dad?" Hummer didn't want him to hang up the phone.

"Yeah?"

"In a week for sure?"

"Well, soon as everything's ready, Hummer. You be good, hear?"

"Yeah. See ya."

"Bye."

Hummer didn't hang up the phone. She sat with the receiver cradled in her lap, feeling no energy to move.

SIXTEEN

On Tuesday morning, Hummer woke early, too early, in spite of having been up late making plans, but nervously got dressed anyway. No one else was up yet.

Then she lay on the bed, squinted her eyes at the dark ceiling, and went over her plans in her head. She remembered the distance on the map between Green Bay and Auroraville. She felt a pang of guilt about that map, torn out of the Peltons' atlas and now folded in the pocket of her jeans, but it couldn't be helped. She had to go home.

The thought jerked her out of a moment's sleepiness, and she felt warm with excitement. By tonight she would be home where she belonged. She would find out what Riley had done with Fox, help her dad with chores, see Leona, call Charlotte. She felt she had been away for years, and that now the sooner she ran away the better. Otherwise she might never get there.

She checked to make sure that the map and money were in her pocket, then, thinking about Florence and

Jack, she found a pencil and a scrap piece of paper. She hoped they wouldn't be *too* worried.

"Sorry for causing trouble!" she wrote. "I like you, just not Green Bay. (I like home best.) You could come visit, and see Fox." Hummer paused, then scratched out "Fox." She wrote in "Mike" instead. After signing it, she added, "P.S. My dad will buy you a new atlas." She hid the note under her pillow. She certainly didn't want anyone to find it before she left.

Still no one else was up. Hummer considered waking Florence, then remembered how early it was. She lay back down on the bed.

She didn't know she'd fallen asleep again until Florence called through her door. "Hummer, up and at 'em." The voice became louder, and Hummer realized Florence had cracked open the door. "Oh, you've dressed already. Ready for breakfast?"

"The important thing," Florence explained later, "is not to get separated. But if we do, we'll just plan to meet at the big fountain in the center of the mall." She looked at Hummer, misinterpreting her look of apprehension. "Don't worry a bit, it's the easiest thing in the world to find. I'll show you as soon as we get there."

As it turned out, they entered at the fountain. Hummer liked the mall right away, even with its crowds of people flowing in and out of shops. She needed some jeans, and to be buying them herself with her own money just like all the people at school did, well, it seemed very exciting. But she had to get home.

138

She slipped away from Florence in a shoe store. They were partially separated, and Hummer simply waited until Florence's back was turned to creep out. Then she ran and skipped her way among the people in the hallway to the first exit she found, then ran out into the parking lot.

Hummer wove her way through the vehicles, making for the crowded street. Almost right away she saw a taxi cab, but she waved too late.

When she saw the second one, she waved with both arms, making sure the driver saw her. It stopped. Hummer opened the passenger side door to slide in.

"Where to, miss?" the taxi driver asked, already shifting into first gear.

"Auroraville, please."

"What street is that?"

"It's not a street, it's a place," Hummer clarified. "Near Waukau."

He pressed the clutch in again. "You sure you know where you're going?"

"Um hmm," Hummer replied, getting nervous. "Auroraville, where I live." She remembered the map, smoothed out the wrinkles, and handed it up to him. "See?" she said, pointing it out to him.

He looked at it, grunted, and handed the map back. "We don't go outta town, miss."

Hummer thought that maybe the driver thought she couldn't pay. She pulled the forty dollars from her back pocket, unwadded the bills, and displayed it to him. "I have money," she told him. "Where could you go for that much?"

"You need a bus," he said. "Not a taxi. Do you want to go to the bus station?" he asked.

"Yes, please," Hummer said.

The bus station turned out to be more complicated than Hummer had hoped. It was big, with two stories, and a lot of people waiting on benches. She went to one of the counters. "I need a ticket to Auroraville, please," she said.

"Auroraville," the lady repeated, and looked down a long list. "None of our buses go to Auroraville." She looked up at Hummer expectantly, but Hummer didn't know what to say after that. "What's the next closest city to Auroraville?" the lady suggested.

"Waukau," Hummer answered. "Do any of the buses go to Waukau?"

One of them did.

Hummer seemed to be the only person without luggage on the bus. She sat in the front seat, to be sure not to miss her stop, and stayed awake the whole ride. Other passengers slept, or talked, but Hummer watched out the window. It took four hours, by the time the bus had stopped and started and made detours. In Waukau, the bus stopped in front of the ice cream shop, and Hummer was the only person to get out.

She stepped into the dazzling sun, amazed to have gotten from one place to another on her own. She felt she could do anything she wanted, or go anyplace.

140

What she wanted now was to find Fox. Hummer walked down Waukau's one main street, past the auction house, and onto the road toward Riley's. She walked fast. In the heat she was sweating, but she didn't care. She didn't even stop at the truck stop for a Coke as she passed it.

She was only a little past the restaurant when a blue Duster passed her on the road, honked its horn, put on the brakes, and backed up.

It was Junior. He pushed open the passenger door, smiling and saying, "Hop in. Where's your horse?"

Hummer slid into the front seat and slammed the door behind her, smiling at his joke.

"I didn't expect that to be you," Junior said. "Heard you were out of town."

"I was. Junior, do you think you could take me to Riley's?" They were at the corner.

Junior drove that direction without answering. But Riley wasn't at home. Hummer didn't see Fox in the pasture, and Junior said, "Truck's not here." Hummer knocked on the door anyway. No answer. She wondered where Fox could be. Riley never would have sold her. She knew that. She didn't let herself think that he would.

"He's been real busy lately," Junior said. "Out driving the back roads all the time. Hasn't really been at the truck stop much." Junior backed out of Riley's driveway. "Maybe we can find him."

They checked the Old Durkey Place, and Hummer

141

saw tire tracks and hoof prints, but no Riley. "They can't be Fox's tracks," Hummer told Junior. "Riley could never ride her." But they looked like Fox's tracks.

"We'll head out to Trump Lake," Junior said.

They bumped along the narrow dirt road out to the pavement to get around Myrtle Creek, crossed the bridge, and headed into the woods again. No tracks this time. Hummer hung her hand out the window, pushing against the wind with it, then stuck her head out to blow the hair out of her face.

"Sure is hot," Junior said, then, suddenly interested, "Lookit there."

Hummer could see a cloud of dust coming and a horse cantering along in it. "It's Fox!" she shouted. She could see Riley's pickup in the dust, and a rope hanging through the window attached to the mare. She bounced once on the seat and put her head out the window again to get a better view.

Junior pulled the Duster into the weeds off the road. "Looks like he's exercising her."

Hummer could see Fox's shining eyes now and the sheen of sweat on her coat. She was still cantering. Hummer untangled herself from the safety belt as fast as she could, practically falling out of the car door.

"Fox, it's me," she called, and then waved at Riley with both arms as she'd done to get the taxi. She ran toward Fox.

The pickup slowed down, and Fox arched her neck into the halter in protest, cantering sideways. Riley let go of the rope. Hummer saw Fox coming toward her in a haio of dust, the lead rope dangling and dancing. The end of the rope found its way into Hummer's hand, and Fox was trotting circles around her, snorting and snuffling into her face. Hummer hugged Fox's neck, feet dancing to keep out from under Fox's, and then, with a hand on the mare's high crest, trotted back with her to Riley's truck. He sat with the door open, legs hanging out the side.

"Riley, she looks beautiful!" Hummer called to him, then circled Fox around the open truck door. The mare finally stood still, blowing quietly.

Riley put a hand on Hummer's head. "I thought you weren't gonna be home for a couple more days."

"I couldn't stand it, so far away. I was scared you might sell Fox."

Riley spit his tobacco. "What would I go and do that for, just before the trail ride?"

"The trail ride?"

Riley grunted.

"We're going on the trail ride?"

"Well, I ain't been killing myself leading this horse around these woods for nothing." Riley was grinning, showing his empty gums.

"Riley!" Hummer grabbed the hand on her head and held it.

Riley slid stiffly down from the truck seat. "Ain't afraid to hug an old man, are you?"

Hummer wrapped her arms around Riley and pressed her face into his tobacco-smelling shirt, shaking her head.

SEVENTEEN

Hummer followed Virgil through the porch and into the house, remembering not to hold her breath. Fresh paint and plaster dust were all she could smell.

Virgil pointed to the empty space beside the stove where the refrigerator used to be. "New fridge ought to be in tomorrow. It's gonna be white." The floor was covered with several green and white rugs.

Hummer couldn't believe how big the house seemed. The ceilings were high and the walls far apart and everything echoed. She'd never noticed it was so big before. "It's so clean," Hummer said aloud. "Like it's our house but it's not." It seemed strange not to see Leona.

They walked into the empty living room. The plaster walls had been sanded down to a rough powdery finish, and the floorboards showed scraps of tar paper and foam that used to be beneath the carpet.

"I'll pick up some furniture at an auction," Virgil said. "Everything stunk. So we hauled her all down to the dump. About the only piece of furniture I held onto was that favorite rocking chair of your ma's. Thought she wouldn't wanna let that go." They climbed the stairs, Virgil in the lead.

The windows in Hummer's bedroom were open as usual, and the sun shone through them. There was a new pink rug on the floor.

"Your room was the only clean spot in the whole place," Virgil said, twisting his cap around backward on his head.

Hummer already knew that.

"Everybody that helped move, Ernie and Elsie, Ethel, Harlow, and everybody, they all noticed it."

"They did? Did they help a lot?" she asked. She sort of hoped they hadn't.

"Well. I didn't really want help at first," Virgil explained, grimacing. "But I wanted you back and they just assumed I'd be needing them. Ernie showed up with a nice big trailer, for hauling stuff down to the dump."

"They didn't, I mean, they weren't –" Hummer didn't know how to say what she meant, but Virgil understood.

"They didn't say a word against your ma. Not one word. All they mentioned was how clean your room was."

Hummer shuffled her bare feet in the rug, feeling luckier and luckier all the time. "I'll keep it clean," she said. "I'll keep the whole house clean." Hummer smiled, trying to show Virgil how happy she was, and then noticed a taut wire strung across the wall.

"What's that?" she asked.

"Likely you'll have some ribbons pretty soon," Virgil said. "I was just looking ahead. And see here?" He gestured to a newly built shelf. "You could put your horse trophies up here." He looked at Hummer to see if she'd like that.

She was crying. She couldn't help it.

"Aw, now, what's wrong?" Virgil took Hummer's hand and sat down on the bed. "Come here." Hummer sat down beside him.

Hummer couldn't talk and cry at the same time, so she had to wait a few minutes before speaking. "How come luck is either all good or all bad?" she asked. "Last week I thought I was the unluckiest person in the whole world, and now all of a sudden I have all this. And I'm going to win horse trophies." She grinned, wiping her wet cheeks with her palms and feeling silly. "Maybe."

"Here." Virgil offered Hummer the ends of her own hair to dry her face with, and she began giggling.

"Don't blow your nose in it," he said.

Hummer smiled. She couldn't wait to sleep in her bedroom that night. Or to hang pictures of Fox someday, or put ribbons on the wire.

"I wanted to have everything all ready by the time you came home," Virgil said.

146

"It turned out good this way," she said. "I still had lots of surprises."

Virgil smiled, twisting his hat around his head once. "I'm glad you're home, only next time try not to scare everybody half to death, would you?"

Hummer nodded. But she knew there wouldn't be a next time. Her dad had already called Yvonne and the Peltons to straighten everything out, and they were going to mail the bundle of clothes she'd left behind.

Yvonne and Bernie Poll would come look at the house again, but this time, Hummer knew, they would think it was a fit place for her to live.

The house felt empty without Leona around. Hummer missed her, but she didn't miss the garbage, that was for sure.

Hummer heard Riley's pickup pulling into the driveway, and she ran down the stairs, two at a time, to meet him.

"Stopped by the auction," Riley said when he saw her. "Bought us some gear for next weekend." He nodded to a long, heavy rope coiled in the bed of the pickup.

"To tie her up with?" Hummer asked.

"It's a picket line. You string it between two trees, then tie the horse's lead rope to that. That way they have a little room to move." He held out something that looked like a long funny rope net. "Know what this is?"

"No," Hummer told him, taking the thing in her hands, looking at it.

"Hay bag," Riley said. "See," he pulled it open, "you stuff it full of hay, close it like this," he yanked the drawstring around the top, "and hang it from your picket line. So Fox don't have to eat off the ground."

Hummer smiled at Riley and experimented with the hay bag. She still could hardly believe she was going on the ride, much less getting new equipment for it. "Thanks," she said.

Hummer jumped up to sit on the hood of Riley's pickup.

"Next week now, you know how much to ride?" Riley asked.

Hummer nodded. It was on her schedule. "I don't ride on Friday at all, the other days about five miles or so, taking it real easy. Is that what you still want me to do?"

"That's right. We want her so bursting with energy by Saturday that when you finish that fifty miles she'll want to turn around and go back. Right?"

"Right," Hummer said.

"Look who's coming," Riley said, looking down the road. "The little gal who's always at the truck stop."

It was Mary Lou. Even though they lived on the same road, Hummer rarely saw her, unless she was walking by on her way to the store or something. She didn't expect it when Mary Lou stopped at the end of her driveway. "Hi, Hummer," Mary Lou called out.

"Hello," Hummer said carefully.

"I better be going," Riley said, but Hummer didn't get off his hood so he didn't start the engine just yet.

"I'm just going to the store," Mary Lou said. "I saw you sitting there."

Hummer didn't know what to say, so she bounced the backs of her boots against the truck tire a few times.

"I saw Charlotte and she told me all about you going on a long horse race. She said she's going with you."

"Um hmm. It's next weekend."

"Well, good luck."

"Thanks."

"Well, bye."

"Bye."

"I see you in the truck stop sometimes," Mary Lou went on. "You should come over to play the video games next time you're there."

"I might," Hummer said, kicking the tire again.

"Well, bye."

"Okay. Bye."

They watched Mary Lou walk away again before Hummer jumped off the hood and Riley started the engine.

"Don't like video games much, huh?" he said when Hummer looked into his open window.

"I'll see," Hummer said.

Riley took a moment to break into a toothless smile, then shifted into reverse.

EIGHTEEN

OAK REST was all the sign on the road said, but inside, past the main gate and down the curving driveway, white block letters on the front of the huge brick building read OAK REST MENTAL HOSPITAL. Hummer shivered and understood for the first time that it was true. Her ma was in an institution.

Together, Hummer and Virgil walked the big old rocker out of the back of the truck, Virgil gripping it by one arm and Hummer by the other. The chair had been Virgil's idea. "It was her favorite thing in the whole house," he'd said. "It'll make her feel right at home."

Hummer could still detect the scent of vinegar in the pores of the chair, but the vinegar had done its job; that was all she could smell.

They carried the chair along the sidewalk and together eased it through the wide door of the empty waiting room, breathing with relief as the cold of the air conditioning hit them. Virgil nodded his head toward a wall where they could let the chair down, and then he moved toward the secretary's window. His hand hovered for a moment over the little please-ring-for-service bell. He turned and sat down instead.

"She'll be back in a minute," he said. "No need to bother her."

Hummer didn't sit down right away, but stood in the center of the waiting room, looking around. Everything was big and quiet and clean, like it had all been dipped into boiling water. Finally, she plopped herself into Leona's chair and began rocking. She felt strange. She looked around at the pale blue walls and the receptionist's window, then stared at the pile of old magazines on the round center table. She rocked a little faster and wondered how it felt to be crazy.

Then Hummer had a terrible thought. "Dad?"

Virgil turned a magazine over in his hands and looked up.

"What do you think Ma's going to do when she sees this chair?"

"I dunno." Virgil looked at Hummer more closely, as if he wondered what kind of answer she was fishing for. "Say thanks or something."

"I just mean, what if it starts making her worse again? What if she starts rocking too much, and . . ." Hummer remembered how sometimes when Leona got started rocking her eyes would glaze over, and she'd stare and stare, like she was in some other world. Hummer shuddered.

"Well, I dunno as something like a chair would make her worse." He hesitated. "Would it?"

"You know that time Ma locked herself in the bathroom? Just before that, when you and me went out to eat, Ma was rocking and rocking. She wouldn't even look at me." Hummer brushed her hair from her eyes. "Ma was sucking her thumb and rocking the chair, like, like a . . ." Hummer was thinking, like a little baby, but she couldn't get the words to come out of her mouth. Suddenly it seemed like the worst thing in the world to give the chair to Leona.

Finally, Virgil said, "Doggone if I never thought of it like that. Like putting a calf back with the cow just before she's weaned, and you have to start all over again." He squinted at Hummer and then smiled at her. "Good thing I got you along," he said.

Hummer didn't know what to say to that, but just then a woman's face peered out of the office window. "Didn't hear you come in," she said politely. "You could have rung the bell, you know."

Virgil went to the window, his hands dug into his pockets, told her their names, and that they were there to visit Leona Ensing.

"One moment please," the woman said. She looked through some papers, then disappeared again.

"She's got to ask a doctor about it," Virgil told Hummer, "and then a doctor will come and take us to see her." Virgil had already visited Leona several times while Hummer was at the Peltons.

"Dad? What are we going to do about the —" Just then another door opened and a man dressed in white came in. Hummer didn't finish. The outside door opened and a couple came in, bringing with them a waft of warm air.

"Nice to see you again," the doctor said to Virgil. He held his hand out to Hummer. "You must be the daughter I've heard so much about. Well, let me tell you, your mom's coming along, but she's going to need your help. I'm glad to see you could make it."

Hummer shook hands with him, feeling shy. She knew he was a psychiatrist instead of an ordinary doctor because Virgil had told her. She followed her dad through the door the doctor held open, glancing back at Leona's chair. It looked as if it belonged there. She suppressed a giggle as a man sat down in it. Then the door closed.

"Did your dad tell you that you're going to come in with him once a week for counseling?"

Hummer nodded. She felt relieved that someone was going to help.

"We want you to know what to do when your mother is back home so that we're solving more than just symptoms here. We think that you can be a real key in helping her get better."

Hummer couldn't tell if the doctor really believed Leona would get well, or if he was just saying it to be nice.

Now they entered an elevator, and Hummer pushed herself against the wall on one side. "What's wrong with her?" she asked shyly.

The doctor looked at her. "Mental illness is hard to

understand," he said. "Long names aren't much help. The question is why, and then what to do about it. That's what we're going to work on."

Hummer decided that that was a long form of "I don't know," but she didn't mind. After all, it *was* confusing. She was just glad somebody was doing something.

The elevator doors opened smoothly, so Hummer and Virgil followed the doctor out. They were in a wide hallway with open doors on either side. Hummer could see televisions in some of the rooms, and couches. She had to keep reminding herself that it wasn't a regular hospital. People's heads were sick, not their bodies.

"Ma?" Hummer saw Leona sitting on a couch. Her hair was clean and shiny and combed, and she wore a new dress, and, for a moment, Hummer thought Leona was better. She thought she'd turn around smiling, asking Hummer if she'd keep the house neat just until she got back. "Ma, we're here," Hummer called.

Leona didn't turn.

Virgil looked at Hummer, and the doctor looked at Virgil.

Leona still didn't turn around. She began rocking herself. Hummer walked to the front of the couch and touched Leona's shoulder. "Here I am," she said again.

It was a long moment before Leona responded, as though she had to travel a long distance. Then her eyes met Hummer's. She smiled.

"Want me to brush your hair?" Hummer asked.

Leona's hairbrush was sitting on the arm of the couch.

"Sure, dolly," Leona said.

Hummer drew the brush through her mother's clean hair, thinking how nice it smelled. "I really don't mind," she explained. "When you come home, I'll brush it every day."

NINETEEN

The morning of the competitive ride dawned cool and clear, and Hummer woke shivering with anticipation. "Charlotte!" she whispered.

"Ummmm." Charlotte pulled the sleeping bag up to her chin. Her eyes were closed.

"Charlotte, wake up. It's here. It's about to happen."

"What is?" Charlotte opened her eyes.

"Fox and me. I mean, the ride. Shouldn't we be up?"

Hummer could hear a trailer door slam and a horse nicker. More horses began whinnying. Another trailer door banged, and Hummer heard the sound of grain being rationed. So did Fox. She nickered and circled on her picket rope.

Hummer untangled herself from the sleeping bag as fast as she could and pulled on her clammy jeans in the dark front of the horse trailer. Her socks were damp too, and there was straw in one boot, but she tugged them on and ran out to Fox.

Fox nickered again, pulling forward against her rope, her chest heaved outward and her neck high. "I'm

156

here, Fox," Hummer told the mare, then stroked her face. Fox was more interested in being fed.

Hummer ran to the horse trailer again and scooped grain into Fox's bucket. Fox pushed her nose into the feed, sighing with pleasure. Hummer took a deep breath.

She knew the mare was ready for the ride. The day before, when they'd first arrived and gone through the vet check, two veterinarians had worked on Fox at once, making sure she was fit to run the race. One took the mare's pulse and respiration, looked into her mouth and eyes, and tested for dehydration, while the other felt down her legs and picked up her hooves. Hummer had to trot Fox in circles for them so they could check her movement, but they found nothing wrong.

When the vets were done, Hummer stood on a big scale, holding her saddle and bridle to be weighed. She was classified as a junior lightweight, then given a jersey to wear. The jersey had the number 104 in big numerals, both front and back.

Hummer remembered the jersey now and felt a surge of pride as she took it out of the tack box. She tied it over her sweatshirt. She brushed Fox while the mare ate, trying to remember everything she'd learned the night before. A meeting had been called in front of the mess tent to inform competitors about the trail and rules.

A lady in a red polka-dot cap handed out plastic-coated mimeographed maps to all the riders.

"The trail is well marked with blue paint," she began, "and as you can see from your maps, it crosses itself once. That should be the only point of confusion and won't be confusing at all since we all have maps. Remember, the mileage will be posted every five miles; you'll always know approximately where you are.

"The biggest hills are about fifteen miles from the start of the ride," she pointed to that area on her own map, held up high, "and there will be two designated places to water along the way, indicated by X's."

Hummer found the two X's on her own map.

"The first is a natural watering hole; we'll meet you with water at the other. Make sure you each give us a marked pail, so you can identify your own as quickly as possible. There will be no community drinking. No pail, no water. We should have enough helpers so that no one will be held up here."

Charlotte touched Hummer's arm and smiled. She and Riley would be on the work crew.

"At two unspecified locations along the way you'll go through vet checks. You all know about the vet checks. Each horse will be held up for ten minutes; longer if his recovery isn't good. It's okay to dismount, rub down legs, whatever you need to do. Any horse that takes longer than twenty-five minutes to recover normal pulse and respiration will be pulled from the ride." She flipped the hat from her head and looked around to see that everyone understood.

She put the hat back on, then pointing to her map again, explained, "Around the thirty-five-mile point you'll run into swamp. The trail is sound, with a few wet spots, but don't get off to the side or you'll bog down.

"There's a bridge here at forty miles, and a paved road to cross at forty-three. It shouldn't be bad, but we'll have a man out watching for traffic.

"Remember, riders, you are to be mounted all the time you're moving forward. No jogging alongside the horse. We'll have spotters along the way, checking off numbers, so if you see somebody sleeping in the bushes, shout your competitor number at them." She grinned.

"We'll send the first rider off at seven o'clock sharp; then another one every sixty seconds, in the same order you arrived at the check-in today. Everyone knows the line-up, right?"

The riders assented. Riley, Hummer, and Charlotte had arrived at camp early, so Hummer would be the seventeenth rider out. There were eighty-some riders, altogether.

"Looks like the weather will be fair, not over seventy-five degrees. We'll let you know the ride speed by seven o'clock."

Hummer knew that for hot weather they might slow the ride to eight miles per hour, for cool or rainy weather, push it up to twelve. She hoped they'd pick ten miles per hour. At ten miles per hour, the mathematics came out even. She'd have thirty minutes to get between each mileage marker, five hours to complete the ride. It seemed simple.

Hummer knew it wasn't really simple, it was just that

she'd ridden and practiced and rehearsed until it seemed simple. Now she wanted to get on with it.

She pulled off Fox's red sheet, which was dirty on one side from where she'd been lying. By the time Hummer had Fox groomed to a high sheen, Riley and Charlotte were up, then Charlotte and Hummer brought breakfast for them all from the mess tent. Caterers had prepared bacon and eggs and pancakes, but Hummer was too excited to eat much. She drank a cup of bitter coffee, gulped down some eggs, then began warming Fox up.

She led Fox back and forth along the two-track in front of the campsite, then around and around the horse trailer. Riley and Charlotte sat on the trailer fender, watching. Each time Hummer passed Riley, he gave her some new piece of advice.

"The first vet check," he asked, "any idea where it'll be?"

Hummer had no idea.

Riley had the map, so he pointed to it. "I'm willing to bet it'll be at the top of one of these first hills. Since there'll be two vet checks, the first one oughta be about that far in."

Charlotte nodded enthusiastically, excited that he'd figured it out.

"They'll want to stop you where they know the horses are all working hard, too," Riley added. "That's another reason I think it'll be at the top of the hill. Might be a good idea to walk her a quarter mile or so before that point, to give her a better chance."

160

Hummer led Fox in another broad circle, then walked past Riley again. "Take the sponge from your tack box," he said. "Tie it to your saddle, and, when you get to the watering places, rinse her legs down."

Other people were warming their horses up now too, up and down the camp, and Hummer knew it was getting close to starting time. Fox was plenty warm by now, but Hummer wanted to make sure. She led her around the trailer one more time.

"Don't forget to drink plenty of water yourself," Riley warned. "No use having the horse in perfect health if you come in dehydrated."

"I think we ought to saddle her," Charlotte said.

"Wear your cap, in case it gets too hot," Riley added. "We don't want you getting overheated."

Riley held Fox's lead rope. First Hummer and Charlotte smoothed the mare's coat one last time with the finishing brush, then gave each saddle blanket a good shaking before squaring it over Fox's withers. Next the saddle went on and Hummer fastened the cinch.

"I should see you at least once out in the woods," Riley said. "Don't know what I'll be doing, but I'll be out there somewhere."

"Me too," Charlotte said. She tied the sponge to one of the latigo straps on Hummer's saddle.

"Don't push too much at the beginning," Riley said, "but remember; the hills and the swamp are going to slow you down. Plan for that."

Hummer slid the bridle onto Fox's head now, fastening the throatlatch and stroking the mare's face.

161

"I'm putting the lead rope on your left side." Charlotte waved it in the air to show Hummer, then tied it next to the sponge. She looked at Hummer's watch and announced, "Two to seven."

Hummer pressed her face into Fox's neck. The mare smelled wonderful and warm and grassy. Hummer sighed with excitement. Horses and people alike were now gathered at the start of the trail. The polka-dot-capped lady stood with one foot propped on a straight-backed chair, talking to a man on a horse. She had a stopwatch in one hand.

Hummer stopped Fox at the edge of the group, looking back for Riley. Riley was shuffling along beside a man leading a gray mare, and when they got close, he turned to Hummer. "Ten," he announced.

"What?" Hummer asked.

"Today's speed. Ten miles per hour."

"Really?" Hummer couldn't believe her luck. Now it would be easy.

"All set?" somebody said loudly, and Hummer realized the first rider was about to leave. The woman in the hat made the stopwatch click. "You're off."

The first horse, a heavyset chestnut, moved off in a swinging trot. The woman on his back did not look back at the group as she disappeared down the trail into the woods.

An assistant with a yellow legal pad on a clipboard called out competitor numbers. One by one, the horse and rider teams trotted down the trail.

When a boy on a big brown and white pinto pony moved up to the line, Charlotte whispered to Hummer, "I think that's the only pony."

"He doesn't look very old," Hummer said.

"The pony?"

"No! The boy."

"Look; he's with his mom." Charlotte pointed to a woman on a pinto horse watching the boy. Just then the stopwatch clicked and the pony began jogging easily down the trail, the boy looking back. At the turn, he stopped the pony and waited. "See," Charlotte added.

They both looked up as the woman getting ready to go answered somebody's question. "Travis is nine years old," she said. "His pony's in better shape than Concho, here. I hope I can keep up." The people around her laughed, then she went cantering down the trail to join her son.

"The pony's got such short legs," Hummer commented.

"But just think, he doesn't weigh as much either," Charlotte replied. "That helps make up for it."

"Plus that kid doesn't weigh much," Hummer added.

Another horse and rider trotted from the starting line, and Hummer gave a shiver of anticipation. It was almost her turn.

"Fox doesn't have to carry much weight, either," Charlotte assured her. "She'll do fine."

At last the palomino mare in front of Fox swished out

of sight, and Hummer found herself waiting at the line. Charlotte checked the cinch for Hummer one last time and gave her a leg up. "Do good," she said.

"Have fun," Riley told her, coming up from behind and patting Fox on the rump.

Fox pulled down at the reins and stepped sideways, responding to Hummer's sudden anxiety. Hummer thought she would burst with excitement if she didn't leave immediately. She watched the second hand of her watch tick painfully around the face.

Finally the woman in the polka-dot hat clicked the stopwatch, nodded at Hummer, and Fox was off.

The mare cantered in the single-track dirt trail following the hoof prints of the other riders. Hummer looked at the trail and then back at the group, waving. The trail made a U-turn, and the camp disappeared.

Hummer hugged Fox's neck, smiling and leaning forward into the whipping ends of Fox's mane. She felt exhilarated by the sound of Fox's pounding hooves, and, knowing full well they were starting too fast, urged Fox even faster. When the mare slowed of her own accord to a fast trot, Hummer posted and smiled into the woods.

The trail was beautiful. The early morning sun shone through the trees in long crisscrossing patterns of light and shadow. The narrow path snaked one way and then the other, so Hummer had to pay attention, ducking branches and keeping her knees from bumping against tree trunks. Hummer could hardly believe that in five hours she would have ridden through fifty miles of all new trail.

Eventually Hummer could hear, but not see, the rider in front of her. No one came from behind, though she knew several more must have started by now. Fox cantered again, and the tail of the palomino swished into sight. The long blond ponytail of the woman matched the color of her horse's tail, and swished with the same rhythm.

When Fox and Hummer neared, the woman twisted backward in the saddle. "Are we lost yet?" she asked.

The trail was marked too well for anyone to get lost. "Not yet," Hummer said, "I hope."

"Well, follow me and we'll end up in a swamp somewhere for sure. I do it every time."

"Look out!" Hummer warned, and the woman ducked a small branch. Just then the trail burst out onto a two-track. Her horse turned in the direction of the blue trail markers without seeming to have instructions. Hummer knew in an instant that she probably never got lost. "Have you done this before?" Hummer asked.

"Once in the rain – I mean an all-day dogs and cats downpour – and once when it was a hundred and three degrees."

"Really?"

"Trail riders are crazy people, they say."

Hummer smiled. She stroked Fox's neck, feeling warmth but no sweat. Soon Fox was alongside the palomino on the two-track, then pulling at the bit to go

165

again. "See ya," Hummer said. "She's in a hurry."

Fox cantered again, her tail arched nearly over her back. Hummer saw the blue paint just in time to turn Fox up a steep bank onto a single track. Fox puffed air at the top of the bank, then zigzagged down the steep incline.

Around another curve, Hummer took in her breath when she saw a black pool of water, bulging frog eyes poking up through the leaves floating at its edges. The trail wound so near its edge that Hummer could see her own split-second reflection in the dark water. Then it was gone.

The trail wove in and out of a birch grove, then around the side of a valley. At one point it met up with an old railroad grade, the two downward sloping banks on either side growing with wild grape vines. Hummer didn't see the spotter in the shade of a big maple tree until Fox shied at him. He waved a hand at her and checked her number off in his notebook.

Fox veered around a sharp curve, close to a tree, and Hummer had to pull a leg up quickly. Then she saw the first mileage marker. It was a square of white cardboard stapled to a tree. It said FIVE in big letters. Hummer was early. It had taken her twenty-four minutes instead of thirty. Now she'd have a chance to let Fox walk before the big hill.

When the ten-mile marker came, Hummer timed it as carefully as she could. She and Fox kept trotting steadily. Hummer hoped that every six minutes they rode exactly one mile. After twenty-four minutes she pulled Fox down to a walk. The mare lowered her head, relaxed, and stepped out in swinging strides. She was damp with sweat, but soon her breathing slowed. Hummer hoped the hill would be soon. She didn't want to lose too much time walking.

When it did come into sight, Hummer saw it wasn't as steep as she'd thought it would be. The bottom was deep sand, though, from where motorcycles had dug it up. Just as Hummer checked her cinch and headed Fox into the sand, the palomino came trotting up.

"Back again," was all the lady said as she tightened her own cinch and followed Fox.

Hummer leaned as far over Fox's neck as she could, feeling the mare's straining muscles. There wasn't a vet check at the top of the hill after all, but a narrow trail that wound along the top of a ridge. Hummer let Fox pause to catch her breath, then they trotted along the trail. Soon it cut sharply downhill again, so steeply that Fox swayed from side to side, sliding downward in the sand with each step.

"That wasn't so bad," the blond-haired lady commented at the bottom. Then they both turned a corner and saw the real hill.

Hummer held Fox back a moment. It seemed to her that she was looking almost straight up. The path was hard dirt now, not like the sand of before. She looked at the other lady.

"Better give her a breather halfway up," the lady advised.

Fox began climbing again, pushing mightily with her

hindquarters, neck stretched forward and straining. Hummer lay almost flat over Fox's mane. She concentrated only on what she could see directly in front of the mare's feet. Halfway up they did pause, and now Hummer could see some horses and people gathered at the top. This must be the vet check. She let Fox catch her breath before she pushed her forward again.

Fox had barely stopped climbing when she was surrounded. A vet held a stethoscope in front of Fox's girth, another counted her breaths, someone else held a stopwatch. Hummer didn't have to do anything. The chestnut who had been first was just starting out again now, and the pinto pony and horse, mother-and-son team were still waiting. The other riders were dismounted, so when a vet told Hummer to move out of the way and wait, she got off too. She stroked Fox's neck, then felt down the mare's legs and checked her shoes. The mare was still breathing hard from the long climb.

"Good Fox of foxes," Hummer murmured to her. "You just rest."

Hummer looped her wrist through the reins, then sat down cross-legged near Fox to study the map. She divided the next thirty-five miles in half to help determine where the next vet check might be. Probably before the main road, she thought, since there would be horse trailers there for any horse the vets pulled from the last leg. Therefore, it would be before the road, and possibly before the swamp, though she wasn't sure about that.

In another four miles, there would be a watering hole for Fox. Hummer realized she was thirsty herself when she thought about it.

"Time," someone said in her ear. The ten minutes were up already. Three people at once surrounded Fox again.

"Having a good time?" a vet asked Hummer as he checked Fox.

Hummer nodded her head enthusiastically. "My best time ever, I think," she said.

"The best time on a trail ride?"

"No. The best time in my life!" Hummer laughed.

He smiled at her. "That's what we like to hear." Then he added, "Take off."

Hummer swung into the saddle, then walked Fox until they were clear of the other horses. Fox broke into an easy trot again.

TWENTY

The second vet check was close to where Hummer had guessed: just before the swamp. She trotted away from it in relief at not having been held over. The big chestnut and the pinto mare had been held back. They were behind her now, and she thought how hard it would be for them to catch up to their places again.

Fox was wet with sweat, so that it foamed along the edge of the saddle blanket and ran down in V's on both sides. "You're so good," Hummer told her over and over.

She hummed a song called "Stewball the Race Horse," thinking that Fox would like it, and posted to the mare's trot. Fox moved easily, though Hummer knew the mare was tired from the way her ears moved: relaxed and to the sides, without popping up continually to look at things. Hummer giggled at this thought. "Ears don't look," she said aloud. Fox's ears flicked back toward Hummer, who laughed again.

The swamp came up quickly. Hummer noticed a few

dead trees, gray and barkless, and then the land on each side of the wide trail dropped off into wet brush. Soon it was flat and marshy. She could smell the sweet, stale smell of muck.

When Fox jerked to a stop, head up and ears straining, Hummer sat suddenly still, trying to hear whatever Fox had heard. She thought it was a wild animal, maybe a deer or something.

Fox began moving again, and when they rounded a curve and dropped into a small dip, Hummer saw with sudden fear what the noise had been. The pinto pony was in the bog. The boy stood partially on the path, one boot in the water, pulling on the ends of the reins.

"Giddup! Giddup! Giddup!" he shouted.

"Whoa, bear," Hummer said. She slid off the saddle on the wrong side, closest the boy, before the mare had stopped. With one elbow looped around her own reins, she grabbed the pony's reins too. "One, two, three, pull!" she said.

The bridle broke.

The two kids looked at each other in panic; the pony squealed and tried to lunge forward. The muck was past his knees.

"He shied at the water!" the boy said. "I tried to make him go through it, but he jumped around."

"Hang on," Hummer said. "I've got a lead rope." She untied it from the left side of her saddle as fast as she could, then made a small loop and slipknot on one end. "I think I can get it over his saddle horn."

Hummer threw the loop toward the pony's saddle twice without luck, and the boy threw it once. Finally she stepped lightly into the wet bog, where she sank to her ankles, and got the loop over the saddle horn. She pulled it tight, then scrambled out again. She was light enough that she didn't sink like the pony.

"Pull him with her," the boy suggested, gesturing to Fox.

Hummer agreed quickly, searched for a place to tie the other end of the rope, and silently thanked Riley for buying her such long lead ropes. As it was, it didn't reach Fox's saddle horn, so she had to tie it to the closest stirrup.

Hummer headed Fox straight down the path, clicking encouragingly. Fox strained. The pony struggled out of the mud and onto the trail. He shook himself.

The kids looked at him and then each other. The boy wiped at his eyes with the backs of his hands. "I was scared," he admitted.

"Is he okay?" Hummer asked.

"I don't know." He moved the pony forward cautiously, with Hummer's lead rope around his neck. "Is he limping?"

"No."

Both the pony and Fox perked their ears up as a big appaloosa came thundering into view. The woman slowed the horse to a fast trot, and called out, "You kids in trouble?"

"Not anymore," Hummer said.

She trotted politely past them, then pushed the horse into a canter again.

"She got held up, once," the boy said. "She's catching up. Mom got held up too."

"Were you going to wait for her?" Hummer asked.

"No. She said keep going, because they might keep her back too long. They might pull her out."

"Let's go together," Hummer suggested. "We have to catch up too, now. A little."

He looked at the pieces of his broken bridle laying in the swamp.

"Here, quick." Hummer unfastened the throatlatch of her bridle and slid it over Fox's ears. "I can do without it if I have to." She didn't wait for him to take the bridle, but shortened the cheekpieces herself and slipped it onto the pony's head. "Some more horses are coming," she said. She could hear them. "Let's hurry."

She scrambled into her saddle and urged Fox into a trot. "Come on," she said. Without the reins she didn't know what do do with her hands for a moment, then put them inside her jersey as if it were a big pocket.

"But how are you going to –" The boy didn't finish, but jumped into his saddle as three horses in a group came into view. "Wait for me," he said.

They cantered up an incline.

"My name's Hummer," Hummer called back to him.

"Mine's Travis." The boy and the pony galloped along next to Fox's large trot. "How are you doing that?"

"I trained her to go without a bridle, but I've never tried it outside the barn. I don't know!"

"Charley would never go without it. He'd stop to eat."

"Is Charley okay?"

"He feels okay. He's tired."

"What time do you have to be in?"

"Five o'clock."

"Five o'clock!" Hummer knew that couldn't be right. He had started a few minutes before her, and she had to arrive into camp at twelve-seventeen.

"Oh. No. See, Mom set my watch funny. As soon as we left, she took it and turned it to twelve o'clock to make it easier. See, at one o'clock we had to be at the ten-mile mark—and we were—and at two o'clock, the twenty-mile mark, at three o'clock, the thirty-mile mark—and we were—but then Mom got held back at thirty-five."

"Hey, that's a good idea, about setting your watch."

"So now we have an hour to get into camp," he added.

Hummer knew they had more than ten miles to go, since they hadn't come to the forty-mile mark yet. Stopping in the swamp had held them both up. "We'll hurry," she said. It amazed her when Fox speeded up almost effortlessly beneath her. "You're a good, good, wonderful, beautiful horse," she said into the dark ear turned toward her.

The trail had been climbing ever since the swamp, but now began a long slow descent. Fox wanted to gal-
174

lop downhill. Slow, slow, slow, Hummer thought with each canter stride, holding the mare to an even tempo. Without her reins, Hummer had to use her body as a brace. "No faster, or you'll fall."

At the bottom of the decline they passed the forty-mile mark, and Hummer let them slow down. "There's a watering place coming up," she said.

"I'm about to croak," Travis answered, holding his hands to his throat.

"Not for you, for them!"

"I know, but Charley will share." He patted the pony's neck. "Won't you, boy?"

As it turned out, there was water for the horses and lemonade for the riders. The buckets were numbered, so the helpers filled them in the order the horses were to come through the checkpoint. Fox's bucket was ready and waiting, and Charlotte herself brought it to Fox.

"You're making it!" she exclaimed. Then she noticed Fox's sleek, bridleless head. "What happened?"

The mare sank her nose into the bucket, blowing with pleasure. She took long gulps.

"Travis broke his bridle trying to pull Charley out of the swamp," Hummer explained. "So I lent him mine." She pointed at Travis and the pony, so Charlotte would know who she was talking about. "We're riding together now. His mother got held back."

Travis grinned at her from where Charley was drinking water.

A woman put a cup of lemonade into Hummer's

hand, at the same time saying, "We'll find you a halter. Someone ought to have an extra halter."

"Would you lookit there!" Riley exclaimed, and Hummer realized he was the one checking off competitor numbers.

"Travis broke his bridle," she said. "I had to give him mine, because his pony won't go without."

Riley sucked in his lips. "Using an old man's trick," he said.

"It's not a trick, Riley!" she exclaimed, feeling pleased that he'd seen her.

Charlotte hurried to get the palomino horse a bucket of water as he came into sight, and meanwhile, another woman came back with a halter. "This is an extra," she said, and slipped it over Fox's head, interrupting the mare's drinking. She attached Hummer's lead rope to the halter, and threw it over Fox's neck. "That ought to be better than nothing." She took the empty lemonade cup back. "Looked like you were doing fine without it," she added.

"Bye, Hummer." Charlotte came running back to give her a quick smile. Then as soon as Fox had finished the water, Travis and Hummer went trotting off again.

"Everyone was looking at you," Travis said.

"They were looking at you too, to see if the bridle fit."

"Not at me, at Charley. I wasn't wearing the bridle!"

They both giggled.

176

"Are you going to have horses when you grow up?" Hummer asked him.

"Nope," Travis answered.

Hummer glanced down at him in surprise.

"I'm going to have ponies," he announced, and they laughed again.

Both Fox and Charley moved out more easily after the water break. They trotted and cantered along comfortably together.

The last five miles were each posted to make last-minute timing easier. The rules gave five minutes leeway either way of the expected time in, so Hummer and Travis decided to stay together and aim as close to Hummer's arrival time as possible. That way neither of them would lose points.

Near the forty-nine-mile marker, Fox stumbled over a log instead of stepping over it, so Hummer pulled her down to a walk with the lead rope and hugged her neck. "Poor Fox," she crooned, feeling bad. "You all right, bear?" Fox walked for a few strides, then of her own accord broke into a trot.

"See, she's okay," Travis said.

"Travis, do you get the feeling they'd keep going until they had a heart attack?" Hummer asked.

"Not Charley. I know. When he gets too tired, he stops."

"Well, Fox would. She'd never stop until I asked her to." Hummer felt a grave sense of responsibility, even more than the time she'd tried to return Fox to Riley.

Then she had guessed what it could be like, being so responsible, but now she knew for sure. She knew how far Fox would go to please her. "Fox of foxes," Hummer crooned. "Almost there." She stroked the mare's neck, worried in spite of being aware that all the signs were good. Fox wasn't breathing too hard or sweating too much, but her legs were tired.

"Look!" Travis said, and Hummer saw the camp over a small rise. A horse whinnied. Fox and Charley both broke into a canter for the last stretch. They were right on time.

TWENTY-ONE

The long silky red ribbon jerked and danced with the motion of the truck. It hung from the rearview mirror, and Hummer read the words on it over and over again. Second place. McKinley Horse Association Fifty-Mile Trail Ride. Junior Division. Second Place. On the back it had a place to write, so Hummer had carefully printed, "Fox and Hummer." She smiled and squirmed deeper into the seat, then glanced sideways at Charlotte, and the other way at Riley.

Riley glanced back at her; Charlotte was asleep. Charlotte held Hummer's trophy loosely with both hands. The trophy had two tall wooden spirals with a horse standing on the top of them. On the bottom, on an engraved silver plate, it said SPORTSMANSHIP.

Hummer could still feel the joy and embarrassment of stepping into the center of the crowd to get her trophy.

"We have one more award to present," the polka-dot-hat lady had announced, after all the other awards had been given, and after Hummer had received her red ribbon.

"Every year, as many of you know, we present a sportsmanship trophy. This person isn't always necessarily a ride winner – last year he didn't complete the fifty miles – but a person who shows outstanding sportsmanship. This year it goes to a young rider who did very well, in spite of some setbacks, and who helped another youngster pull his pony out of the swamp. When the pony broke his bridle, she gave him hers, and finished the ride without one, as any of you riding near her couldn't help but notice." She had looked for a moment at Travis, then at Hummer. "Hummer Ensing, will you come here?"

The crowd clapped. As she received the trophy, Hummer had smiled at the woman with the polka-dot hat, at Travis, at the palomino lady, and all around the circle. Then she had run back to the picket line to show Fox, and to hang the red ribbon from her halter.

Now she thought of the citizenship award the grade school presented every year and which she had never won. She knew the sportsmanship trophy was like that: for people who were good sports. For people who didn't tell lies, for people whom other people liked.

Hummer could feel the heaviness of the trailer behind them, the way it weighed down the back of the truck, and she liked knowing that Fox was so nearby. She could see the tops of her dad's silos now, and the cow pasture.

180

Riley glanced at her again. He looked at the red ribbon too, and then at the trophy. His face crinkled into a smile.

He turned the truck into the driveway. Hummer nudged Charlotte. "We're here," she said.

Together Riley, Charlotte, and Hummer unloaded Fox from the trailer. The mare scrambled out with a clang of hooves on metal, and whinnied a trumpeting whinny. She looked all around the farm, ears up.

Mike whinnied to Fox, and Fox nickered back as Hummer led her through the corral gate. Fox snorted at Mike and snuffled noses with him, then rolled and rolled in the sand.

"Tonight she oughta have a bran mash," Riley told Hummer. Fox loved a warm bran mash.

"And extra grain," Charlotte added.

"And deep straw," Hummer said.

They all agreed.

While Charlotte helped Riley unpack the things from the trailer, the extra hay, tack, buckets, and clothes, Hummer ran straight through the milkhouse and into the parlor. She heard her dad in the grain room above her, so she went through the parlor door, and, holding the ribbon in her teeth and trophy in one hand, began climbing the ladder.

"Dad!" She peered across the floor of the grain room at her dad's rubber boots. A big shovel was pushing grain down the square holes in the floor. The grain poured into chutes that filled the feeders in the parlor.

"Dad, look what I won."

Virgil leaned on the handle of the shovel, his coveralls coated with grain dust. "What've you got there?"

Hummer held the trophy over her head and climbed the last few rungs no-handed. She gave her prize to her dad.

"Sportsmanship," she said. "And this ribbon, for getting second place."

Virgil turned the ribbon over in his hands several times. "Would you lookit there," he said, and turned it over again. "Second place." He read the words on it, then looked at the trophy.

Hummer smiled at her boots.

"Well, I'll be darned. You finished the ride okay?"

"Um hmm."

"Fox did okay? She didn't get too tired?"

"No. She did fine."

"You didn't get too tired?"

"No. Charlotte wants to go next time. With Hawk. In the spring maybe we can both go on a ride."

"Did you sleep okay? You didn't stay up all night talking, did you?"

Hummer giggled. "Yes, we did! Well, not *all* night. It was fun."

He swatted her with the end of her own ribbon, so she giggled again.

"Where's Riley now?" he asked.

"Down there." She pointed out the open grain room door. "I better go help, but wait till I tell you about what happened in the swamp!" She took the ribbon and trophy back from him.

"You can tell me the whole story later. We'll take those into town to show to your ma. She'll be proud, all right."

Hummer nodded and smiled at her dad again as she climbed down the ladder. In the milkhouse, she took a long drink of water from the faucet. Virgil's toothbrush and toothpaste were gone from beside the sink. He didn't live in the barn anymore. The space beside the milk cooler where the cot used to be was now cleanly swept cement.

Hummer hadn't expected to miss those things, but she couldn't help remembering lying in the cot, sick, and what a comfort the sight of the big dewy milk cooler had been. Virgil had held her hand so tightly that night. But now there were the new morning sounds in the house of her dad getting up. He made lots of homey noises, running water and shaving. Hummer woke up happily to these sounds, then waited her turn for the bathroom before going out to help with chores.

She swiped the back of her hand against her mouth, and ran out to help Riley and Charlotte with the rest of the unpacking. She scraped out the back of the horse trailer with a shovel, then closed the doors tight.

"Gonna get cool tonight," Riley commented. He moved toward the open truck door. Charlotte followed him since he was giving her a ride home.

"Bye, Hummer," Charlotte said.

"Bye, Charl."

"See you Saturday!"

"And see you in school!" Hummer could hardly believe school started next week already.

The truck and horse trailer backed out of the driveway. Hummer waved, then slipped through the fence into the pasture with Fox and Mike.

She could hear Riley's truck bumping along the gravel road, with the extra clang of the horse trailer. Virgil walked toward the house, and then the lights came on, one by one. Hummer looked around at the barn where the cows were lined up at the bunker feeder, eating their silage.

The poplar trees in the yard rustled in the slight wind, and Hummer thought that Riley was right, the night would be cool. She promised Fox extra-deep straw in the stall that night and, with the mare's breath still in her hair, slipped between the wires of the fence to move toward the lighted porch.